PHOTO FINISH

The girl screamed. Then she stood up and raked her finger nails across Shayne's cheek. The torn bodice of her dress came open, and she was clinging to him with surprising strength.

There was a noise and a flash bulb went off. Shayne looked up and saw two men grinning at him from the doorway. One of them held a camera—the other an ugly, short-barreled gun . . .

TICKETS
FOR DEATH
Brett Halliday

A DELL MYSTERY

Published by DELL PUBLISHING CO., INC.
750 Third Avenue, New York, N.Y. 10017

Copyright © 1941, by Brett Halliday
Dell ® TM 681510, Dell Publishing Co., Inc.

DEDICATION: To John and Mary Helen

Previous Dell Edition: #387
New Dell Edition
First Printing—July 1965

Printed in U.S.A.

MICHAEL SHAYNE SAT WITH HIS SHOULDERS HUNCHED over the bar at Joe's Joint in downtown Miami, his gray eyes flickering over the crowd with morose disinterest while one big hand warmed a glass of cognac. When Timothy Rourke came toward him with a broad grin, Shayne nodded to Joe. "Set out the bottle and another glass."

The proprietor set a bottle and a two-ounce glass on the bar. Shayne cuddled his larger glass defensively as Tim Rourke flung a long leg over the stool and sat beside him.

Rourke said, "Damned if you haven't got a sweet graft, Mike. I've been trailing you from one bar to another for the last two hours." He filled his glass and emptied it, poured himself a second.

Shayne rumpled his coarse red hair with long knobby fingers, then shoved the bottle beyond Rourke's reach. He said, "I'm not working today," sipping lazily from his wineglass. "What are you trailing me for?"

Rourke folded his arms and relaxed against the bar. "Just a messenger boy, believe it or not. Since you got married your dames come to me when they want to get serviced."

"Do they?"

"Do they what?"

"Get serviced when they come to you?"

Rourke snorted. "They don't want what I can give them. I trail you around to fix up assignations on your behalf.

And Phyllis sitting at home waiting for you. Damn it, Mike, you keep me blushing with shame." Rourke's arm swept out and his thin fingers clutched the cognac bottle.

"If you told me anything that made sense I might buy you a pint bottle with a nipple on it," Shayne said without rancor.

"All right." With his glass filled to the brim for the third time, Rourke gesticulated widely. "So I'm sitting in my office after putting the rag to bed and the phone rings and it's your wife. There's a trusting colleen, you lug. She's got a message for you from a dame and can I find you and deliver it? It's business, she says, and I think monkey business but I don't break her trusting young heart by saying so."

"I'm waiting for the message," Shayne growled. "A few less interpolations would get it off your chest quicker."

Rourke finished his glass and smiled sweetly. He reached in a sagging coat pocket and drew out a slip of paper. "Lucky you married a gal who doesn't know the addresses in this man's town like we do. What kind of business would a doll at the Red Rose Apartments have with you?"

Shayne took the slip of paper from him and spread it out on the bar, frowning at Rourke's penciled scribble: *Miss Mayme Martin, No. 14, Red Rose Apts.* He said, "That's out on Second Avenue, isn't it?"

"As if you didn't know," Rourke scoffed.

Shayne frowned mildly. He folded the slip of paper and put it in his pocket. "Mayme wants to see me, eh?"

"That's the way Phyllis got it over the phone. She said the gal was panting with eagerness. Which one is Mayme? Would it be the little peroxide blonde with the hips?"

Shayne shook his red head and finished his drink. "I'm not socially acquainted with the inmates at the Red Rose."

He pushed his glass aside and nodded to Joe. "Mark that up against me." He paused as he turned away. "Thanks, Tim. I'll see if I can arrange an introduction for you with Mayme while I'm over there."

He took a worn felt hat from the rack on his way out and jammed it down over his bristly hair.

Outside, the air was warm and balmy. It was late afternoon and Flagler Street was crowded with bareheaded, sports-attired visitors. Shayne glanced up at the sky and was surprised to see it overhung with heavy clouds. He hesitated for a moment, then shouldered his way to the curb, got into his shabby roadster and drove east on the one-way street to Second Avenue, where he turned north.

After a few blocks he passed out of the business district and drove through the old residential section of once imposing homes, now made over into furnished rooms and housekeeping apartments.

Beyond, there were newer stucco apartment houses lining both sides of the avenue. He parked in front of one with a rosebush struggling for sufficient sustenance from the sand and coral rock to trail over the trellis arching the entrance. A small sign in the center of the lush green lawn read *No Vacancies.*

Two girls sitting in uncurtained upstairs windows leaned out to watch Shayne go up the walk. He strode into a cool entrance hall with a row of mailboxes on the left. A large lounging-room on the right was unoccupied. Most of the mailboxes had girls' names on them, but No. 14 had no slip in the slot.

A tall, pleasant-faced woman came out of the lounge room as Shayne turned away from the boxes. She had gray hair curled softly back from her face and she wore a sheer white dress. She smiled and asked, "Looking for someone?"

Shayne said, "There's no name on Number Fourteen."

"That's a new girl—Mayme Martin. She moved in today. I believe she's in if you wish to see her."

"I'll go up." He went past the tall woman to a stairway and climbed to the second floor—No. 14 was in the rear. He knocked, and the door was opened immediately.

Bougainvillaea trellised the windows on the west and coco-palm fronds pressed close, dimming the interior of the apartment. A woman swayed before Shayne in the doorway, clutching the knob with white, convulsive fists. Her breath reeked of gin and her face was not pretty. Fear and drunkenness distorted her pale eyes and her skin was pasty-white without make-up. She wore stockings, but no shoes.

The woman waggled her head foolishly and clung to the doorknob as she stared up at Shayne. "You've got the wrong door, mister. I didn't know this place was a joint when I checked in today. Try any of the other doors down the hall and you won't get turned away."

Shayne said, "I'm looking for Mayme Martin."

Her lower jaw sagged open and the tip of her tongue pressed hard against her lower teeth. She threw her head back and squinted farsightedly at Shayne. Terror spread over her face, then went away swiftly as relief came to her eyes. "Are you the detective I tried to phone?"

"The name is Shayne—Michael Shayne." He stepped into the doorway and she let go of the knob, moved aside to let him enter the disordered living-room. An expensive though marred hatbox stood open in the center of the floor. Dresses and slips hung on the chairs, and Shayne pushed a big white straw hat aside to make a place to sit down on the wicker lounge.

Mayme Martin swung the door shut and came toward

him with the exaggerated care of one who is drunk and fully aware of it. "Maybe I better fix us a little drink," she suggested thickly. "I got gin and orange juice in the ice-box."

Shayne shook his head firmly and lit a cigarette. "Not for me, and you don't need any more right now. What did you want to see me about?"

"I'll tell you, Mr. Shayne. I'll tell you right straight out and no beating around the red rosebush. That's the way I am, see? Anybody knows Mayme Martin'll tell you that's the way I am." She swayed back and stumbled over a shoe on the floor, kicked it aside, and said, "Damn."

Shayne got up, took her arm, and helped her to a seat. She giggled delightedly. "Pooped—that's what I am. Pooped to the gills if you want to know. And what if I am? Why shouldn't I get pooped, Mr. Shayne? Nothing like a little gin, I always say, to relax a girl when she's all worn out from moving."

"That's right." Shayne sat back on the couch and stretched long legs out in front of him.

"But it takes money to buy gin," Mayme informed him. "Yes, sir, that's what it takes. I got a bottle in the kitchen and if you want a drink—" She paused to squint at him hopefully.

Shayne shook his head. "Not right now."

The woman wasn't more than forty, he guessed, but her bloated cheeks and unhealthy pallor made her appear much older. Her hair was obviously bleached and recently marcelled, but it was straggly now and she continually pushed damp strands away from her face with wavering fingers. And yet, in her bearing there was a suggestion that under happier conditions she might have dignity and poise.

Shayne again tried to break through her gin-induced fog to learn why she wanted to see him. "Why did you call for me on the phone today? Where did you get my name?"

"I heard them talking about calling you in on the case," she mumbled. "As soon as I heard them talking about you I said to myself, I said, 'Mayme Martin, here's your chance to pick up some easy money for yourself.' Yes, sir, I said, 'You've been a fool long enough. All your life you've been giving away what you might as well get paid for, and this is one time when you're going to cash in while the getting is good.' So I packed up and came right down here to see you, Mr. Shayne."

"All right," Shayne said. "So you're determined to cash in. On what? What have you got to sell me?"

"Not what you think, mister." She opened her eyes wide and smiled cunningly. "I've been around long enough to know there's younger and prettier girls than me on the make. Though there was a time . . . I'm telling you there was a time—"

"I don't doubt that," Shayne broke in. "But what are you selling today?"

"Information, mister. The old inside info. I've got it on tap, see? But it's for sale. I'm not giving anything away. No, sir. I've learned my lesson. What does it get you? Tell me that? What does it get a girl?"

"Information about what?" Shayne asked patiently.

"Oh, you know, all right. Listen, I can crack that case wide open for you. Wide open—" she snapped her fingers feebly—"just like that." She pursed her lips and nodded sagely. "And that's worth money. Don't tell me it isn't."

"What case?"

"Don't try to kid me. The one you're working on."

"I'm not working."

She slitted her eyes and screwed up her face in disbelief. "Don't hand me that line. I know what you think. You think I'm drunk enough so's you can get it out of me without paying for it. That's where you're wrong, mister. I'm drunk all right, but not that drunk. Not by a damn sight. I know what you're working on, and I know what my dope is worth to you. A grand, that's what. A pure grand. And you're going to lay it on the line before I give."

"What case am I working on?" Shayne tried again.

"You know damn well Albert Payson called you in today. Why, it was in the paper. The Cocopalm *Voice* had the story spread all over the front page. Try to deny *that*."

"I'm not denying anything," Shayne said gently. He frowned at the dead cigarette butt between his fingers, tossed it toward a smoking stand in the corner. His right thumb and forefinger massaged the lobe of his left ear while he asked carefully:

"Suppose I am working on a case in Cocopalm? Why should I pay you for information concerning it?"

"Because it's the only way in God's world you'll ever get the straight of it," she assured him promptly.

"But—who pays *me*?" Shayne spread out his big hands. "A grand is a lot of money."

"It's not so much. Not half what it's worth. Why, they're bumping the track for three times that much every night. And they say you always manage to make your fee out of a case."

Shayne shrugged his broad shoulders and stood up. "You might as well be talking Greek so far as I'm concerned. If you've got anything that's worth money, tell me what it is and I'll see you get what it's worth. Otherwise, I'm not interested."

"Oh, no. You don't pull that. Not this time. I've heard

that song and dance before. This time it's going to be on the line before I give, and you'll come to me. I'll be sitting right here holding the lid on until you spread the berries out in front of me."

Shayne said, "Okay. When I decide you've got something worth a grand I'll be around. In the meantime you'd better lay off the liquid diet and take on some raw meat to soak up what you've already drunk." He picked up his hat and went toward the door.

Mayme jumped up and swayed against him. She caught his arm in a surprisingly hard grip, and thrust her face close to his. Her eyes were strangely dilated. "Don't wait too long. Maybe it'll be too late if you wait very long. I'm warning you." A look of cunning passed over her face. "I know I've stuck my neck out and I don't care," she went on, "but I mean to cash in just once before I kick off."

"What do you mean it'll be too late if I wait—too long?"

Mayme shrugged and her body went lax again. "Do I have to draw you a picture?"

"Nothing you've said makes sense," Shayne said irritably. "If you'd give me a few of the pieces—"

He was facing the door and Mayme was looking past him toward the fading light coming in the rear windows. She stiffened suddenly and shrank away, throwing up a hand to shield her eyes. A moan came from between her set teeth.

Shayne whirled. Mayme was pointing a shaky finger at the window, but he could see nothing.

"There! I saw him," the woman screamed. "Oh, my God, if he's found me—"

Shayne strode swiftly to the window and looked out. There was a clear twenty-foot drop, with no fire escape or balcony. The frail latticework supporting the bougainvillaea beside the window would not support a small child. He shook his head and went back to Mayme, saying savagely, "There's no one there. There hasn't been anyone there." He caught her shoulders and shook her. "You'd better tell me what this is all about."

Mayme shook her blondined head stubbornly. She backed away from him and sat down. "Not till the money's on the line. I'm not saying a word. I know it couldn't be him. He wouldn't look for me *here*. Not him." Her shrill laughter pierced the shadowy corners of the room.

Shayne turned away in disgust. "Next thing you'll be seeing pink lizards wearing top hats. Call me when you're sober."

"You're not the only string to my bow. Don't think you are. I got another little trick up my sleeve if you're going to be that way." She giggled drunkenly. "This case has got angles you'll never find out about except from *me*."

Shayne said, "Shake the trick out of your sleeve."

She nodded absently. "All right. I'll do just that." She staggered to her feet and went past him to the telephone.

Shayne lit a cigarette while she flipped the pages, straining her eyes to read the small print. He waited with an expression of curiosity mingled with annoyance to see what she would do next.

Presently she nodded and lifted the receiver in an unsteady hand. She dialed a number and waited, not looking at Shayne, conscious of his presence but aggressively ignoring him.

She spoke into the mouthpiece with a false note of brightness, "This is Mayme Martin calling. Uh-huh. From Cocopalm. But I'm in Miami now. Is this Mr. Max Samuelson?"

Shayne stiffened and pivoted toward her slowly. His lean

face was a study in anger, but he made no move to interrupt the conversation.

"I thought you'd remember me," Mayme Martin was saying. "I met you in Cocopalm last month. Sure, that's right. When you were up to see Ben Edwards about his invention. It's finished now. They say it works perfectly. Naw. The nut still don't want a patent."

She paused, and then her voice took on a fierce note of determination: "Now, you listen to me. I know where those plans are. I know a lot about a lot of things. But I'm not talking, see? There's them that think I don't know what the score is and think they can make a stooge out of me for nothing. But I'm sitting in the driver's seat right now, and I'm staying there until I get my price. All right, come on over, but you'd better bring some cash with you. Nothing else talks to me. Sure. Right away. Number fourteen, the Red Rose Apartments."

She hung up and glanced defiantly at the detective. "There! What did I tell you? He's coming right over."

"That cheap little shyster," Shayne said with acid distinctness. "If you think I'm going to bid against him you're wrong."

Mayme's laugh was shrill. Her eyes glittered with greedy delight. "Shows you don't know what it's all about. What I'm selling Max Samuelson is different from what I'm offering you. Sort of different, that is." She frowned, shaking her head to clear away the fog of perplexity. "What I mean is, you and Mr. Samuelson are on different sides of the fence."

"We always have been," Shayne growled. He hesitated, watching her carefully. "I'll treat you fairly," he urged. "If you'll tell me what you're trying to sell I'll see about getting the cash."

Mayme shook her head cheerfully. She wavered to her feet. "Come back after I make a deal with Mr. Samuelson. I swear I'm not playing you against each other. I got something that's worth a grand to both of you."

Shayne's mouth tightened into a grim line as he fixed three names in his memory: Albert Payson, Ben Edwards, Max Samuelson. He studied Mayme Martin for a moment, then said, "Be careful," softly, and went out.

He was sweating when he closed the door of No. 14. The hall lights had been turned on and as he passed doors which stood ajar, radio music floated into the hall.

A sweet-faced redhead stood in an open door near the head of the stairs. She cocked her head and spoke a soft greeting as Shayne passed. He stopped on the first step and looked back at her. She was no older than Phyllis and she couldn't know much about the life that lay ahead of her. He started to speak and she moved toward him. He turned from her and went on down the stairs and out into the clean coolness of the tropical twilight.

Clouds were banked against the southern sky and a fresh southeasterly wind whipped at his hair. He got into his car and tossed his hat aside, rolled down the windows. Still thinking of the young redhead and wondering whether he was developing a belated social conscience, he muttered "Damn" and swung around to Biscayne Boulevard and south past Bayfront Park. There he turned to the right, then to the left, and parked in front of an apartment hotel on the bank of the Miami River.

Passing through the lobby he nodded curtly to the clerk, then went up three flights in the elevator. Down the hall he stopped before the door of a pleasant corner apartment, opened it, and stopped short just inside the room and whistled in shrill surprise.

A slim, black-haired girl was on her knees struggling with the straps of a Gladstone bag which was packed too full. Two handsome pieces of luggage stood conspicuously on the floor beside her.

Phyllis Shayne looked up from her task and said, "It's high time you came home. Here I have to do all your office work and the packing for the family and you're not even interested enough in your business to let me know where I can reach you."

Shayne said mildly, "Packing, angel?" flinging off his hat and rumpling his coarse red hair. He reached her in six long strides. "Where are we going?"

"To Cocopalm." Phyllis settled back on her trim high heels and let her husband strap the Gladstone. "If I wasn't around to take messages you'd never get a case," she said severely and with a twinkle of pride.

Shayne queried, "Cocopalm?" narrowing his gray eyes at her.

She nodded her dark head emphatically. "We'll have to eat and run. It looks as if it's going to rain little frogs and fishes, and you have an appointment with Mr. Hardeman at seven o'clock sharp. There's barely time to make it. I've got dinner ready."

Shayne echoed, "Hardeman?" in a wondering voice.

"John Hardeman," she elaborated. "He's the manager or something of the greyhound track at Cocopalm. Someone has been cashing counterfeit tickets at the dog track and they're going to have to close it up if you don't do something. So, I told him you'd be up tonight and put a stop to it." She smiled, flushed and radiant, waiting for his approval of the manner in which she had conducted his affairs in his absence.

Shayne snapped the last catch on the bag and stood up

without saying anything. He circled his wife and the packed luggage on the floor to arrive at the built-in wall mirror, which swung out to reveal a completely equipped bar. His angular face was sober and questioning as he poured a drink of cognac. He turned back toward Phyllis with the glass in his hand.

"Now tell me just what happened this afternoon, angel."

She sat flat on the floor looking up at him, her dark eyes deep and serious. "First, about three o'clock a Mr. Albert Payson phoned. I don't think it was long-distance. When he asked for you, I told him in a very businesslike way that I was Detective Shayne's private secretary. He didn't want to tell me anything, but I assured him I took care of the office and received all messages when you were out."

"Never mind the suspense, angel. Who is Albert Payson and what did he want?"

"Oh, he owns the dog track at Cocopalm. He said they wanted you to come up and track down the counterfeiters. I guess Mr. Hardeman didn't know Mr. Payson had already called you because he told me the same thing. I'm positive his call was long-distance from Cocopalm. He was very explicit about your seeing him at the Tropical Hotel at seven tonight." She paused again, counting off the messages on her fingers. "Then there was the message from that girl. I called Tim Rourke and he said he'd find you. I didn't tell Tim about Mr. Payson calling because I didn't think you'd want anybody knowing about it but us."

"Tim found me," Shayne told her soberly. His face grew suddenly hard and his eyes were bleak.

Phyllis sprang to her feet. "Michael," she breathed, "have I made a mistake—saying you'd take the case?"

He smiled and moved his head in quick negation. "Hell,

no, angel. You did exactly right. Only—I wish I'd known about this an hour ago."

"Well, it's your own fault. You didn't telephone me all afternoon." She linked her arm in his and urged him toward the dinette where dinner was waiting.

"Starting tomorrow," Shayne said jovially, setting his glass of cognac on the table, "I'm going to install a broadcasting station so you can tune in on me—"

"We've got to hurry," she interrupted. "Sit down and I'll put dinner on."

"Cocopalm is only thirty or forty miles up the coast. I won't need all those clothes you've packed, particularly the hatbox. I always wear my hat, you know."

"That old hat," she scoffed. "Anyway, the other bags are for me."

"But, Phyl—"

She placed a three-inch rare steak on his plate and surrounded it with French-fried potatoes. "If you think you're going off on a case, darling, and leave me behind to twiddle my thumbs, you're mistaken. It's all arranged. I've reserved a suite at the Tropical Hotel by telephone."

Shayne said, "You do think of everything, angel. If you think it'll be more entertaining to twiddle your thumbs in a Cocopalm hotel suite than here in our apartment, it's okay by me."

She prepared her own plate and sat down. Shayne emptied the cognac glass, then cut into the steak with the relish and gusto of a starving man.

Chapter Two: KNOCK ONCE, THEN TWICE

PHYLLIS WATCHED ANXIOUSLY through the dinette window as heavy clouds obscured the sky and brought dark on early. They ate hurriedly and Phyllis was standing in the doorway with her hat on and ready to go when Michael pushed his chair back and rose from the table.

Rain came down in violent wind-driven torrents as they made a dash for the parked roadster, a blinding semi-tropical deluge accompanied by sheet lightning and rolling thunder. Shayne yanked the luggage compartment open and jammed the bags in while Phyllis hugged a brilliant transparent raincape protectively around her sports frock and white fur chubby.

"Get in and start the motor," Shayne muttered. "I've got to make a stop before I leave town."

"But, Michael—"

"Hurry up, angel. It's important." He slammed the door of the compartment and was seated in the car before she could arrange the dripping cape around her.

"We haven't time to stop anywhere, Michael," she said. "We'll be lucky to get to Cocopalm by seven, and I promised Mr. Hardeman."

Shayne stepped on the starter with his number twelve and pulled out cautiously. He snapped on the windshield wiper and it swung rhythmically back and forth to no avail. The deluge kept the glass opaque and visibility was further obstructed by the reflection of street lights.

"I've got to see your pal Mayme Martin," Shayne told her.

"Why, she's the girl—Watch out, Mike, there's a car!"

"Damn," he said, and swerved to the right. "Never mind. She's probably still too drunk to talk sense."

"You wouldn't have time anyway," Phyllis pointed out in a prim, businesslike voice. "Mr. Hardeman said it was terribly important for you to be there at seven."

"If this keeps up we'll be lucky to get there by morning," Shayne answered sharply. "Okay, angel, first stop is Cocopalm."

"It won't keep up," she consoled him. "You know how it rains here. Flooding everything, and then all of a sudden dust is flying in your face."

Shayne grunted and crept along First Avenue to Flagler, where he turned right and continued on the boulevard. The rain slackened a little, and by the time he reached Grand Concourse there was only a light drizzle. A road sign ahead said: *Speed Limit 35 miles per hr,* and Shayne stepped up to fifty. A few miles farther on the headlights shone upon a dark straight line separating wet pavement from dry. The road sign read: *50 miles per hr.* Shayne pressed on the accelerator and the indicator shot to sixty-five.

Phyllis was strained forward peering through the windshield. She sat back with a sigh and looked at her wrist watch. "It's six-thirty," she said, "and it's twenty-five miles to Cocopalm."

Shayne grinned. "We'll make it with a minute or two to spare."

The broad highway approached the outskirts of Cocopalm along the Atlantic shore, and at the southern edge of town veered off from the north-south highway to strike directly through the business district. To the left of the wide street as they entered the city limits a high board fence enclosed the brilliantly lighted greyhound track. The sport attracted clients from the entire coastal region lying between Palm Beach and Miami.

A band was swinging a march as Shayne drove past. The grandstands were filled with sporting enthusiasts, though the first race of the evening was not scheduled to start for half an hour.

"I'll bet they're parading the dogs," Phyllis cried excitedly, her dark eyes glowing.

Shayne's face was grim. He slowed to forty. "Counterfeit racing-tickets could be a serious problem here," he muttered as he left the track's bright lights behind. "It would be a simple matter to print duplicates for each race and have stooges supplied with them in advance to cash after the race is won. I wonder why someone hasn't thought of it before."

"How would they know which dog was going to win?" Phyllis asked. "Doesn't each ticket have the number of a certain dog printed right on it?"

"Sure. But they could print a whole series of tickets for every race. If each stooge is supplied with all the numbers, all he has to do is wait until the winning number goes up on the board and then discard all his losing tickets and cash the right ones."

"Oh." Phyllis nodded. "No wonder Mr. Hardeman sounded so upset about it. I gathered that it has been going on for some time and they've kept it quiet, hoping the practice wouldn't spread to other tracks. But it has finally got so bad they have to take steps or close the track."

Shayne responded with a glum nod. He was thinking back to Mayme Martin's words. "It wouldn't be difficult to clean up two or three thousand a night if it was worked right," he said, and slowed to thirty as they approached the downtown section of Cocopalm. He stopped for a traffic light, then drove three blocks and pulled up between two rows of gleaming royal palms at the door of the Tropical Hotel.

The place looked like money. A uniformed doorman stared down his nose at the shabby roadster. Shayne snapped, "Get the luggage out of the compartment." He helped Phyllis to shed her wet raincoat, took her hand as she stepped from the car, and grunted sourly, "This is one of those tourist traps where they charge you for drawing your breath. I hope to God my fee at least covers the bill."

Phyllis said, "Pooph," lightly. "You always manage to get along, Detective Shayne, and I adore the service and the luxury of these hotels."

They went into the lobby with Phyllis clinging happily to his arm. At the desk, the clerk admitted that there was a suite reserved for Mr. and Mrs. Michael Shayne.

"Mr. Hardeman is expecting you, sir," he told Shayne. "His number is three-twelve, just down the hall from your suite."

A rack of newspapers caught Shayne's eye as he turned away from the desk after registering. They were afternoon editions of the Cocopalm *Voice,* and a black headline announced: *Miami Detective Called In.*

Shayne paid a nickel for a paper and read it as they went up in the elevator. He swore at a blurred picture of himself, read a sketchy review of the important cases he had broken in past years, and the *Voice* did not hesitate to predict that the gang of counterfeiters would soon be brought to justice.

Pressing against him, Phyllis read the front page and chuckled with pride and delight. Shayne winced inwardly. When they stepped from the elevator a bellboy darted from a service elevator and preceded them to the door, unlocked it to reveal a magnificent living-room with doors leading into a bedroom. After opening the windows, the boy stood politely waiting further orders. Shayne tossed him a fifty-cent piece and he went out.

Shayne threw the newspaper down angrily and muttered, "I don't know why they didn't have the brass band out to meet us. This is a hell of a way to call a private dick in on a job." He strode to the doorway of a large bedroom overlooking the ocean.

Phyllis was unpacking and exclaiming delightedly over the luxurious appointments of the room.

"To hell with all this, angel." Shayne was feeling suddenly uncertain; he'd never gone on a case in this holiday mood before. Finally he strode to the night table and picked up the telephone. "Connect me with room three-twelve."

The phone rang several times at the other end before there was an answer. The voice that came over the wire was thin and harassed. "Yes? Who is it?"

"Mike Shayne—from Miami. I think I have an appointment with you, Mr. Hardeman."

"Can you come to my room right away?"

"Presently," Shayne growled. He looked at his watch. It was one minute to seven.

"Knock once and then twice on my door when you come, Mr. Shayne, so I can be certain it is you."

Shayne said, "Right," and hung up. He stood staring down at the telephone while his thumb and forefinger massaged the lobe of his ear. A questioning look came into his eyes and one bushy brow twitched upward in a V.

Phyllis asked quickly, "Is everything all right? Isn't Mr. Hardeman expecting you?"

Shayne turned his face away from her. The lines on his gaunt cheeks and forehead had deepened into trenches. He said, "Sure, angel. Everything's all right."

"If everything is all right, why are you pulling at your ear?" She went swiftly to him and put her arms around his neck. "You've been acting queer ever since you came home and I told you about this case, Michael. Are you angry because I took it without consulting you?"

He lifted her chin with a broad palm and kissed her lips. "I'll be all right as soon as I find out what's going on and what to expect." He put her gently aside and went into the living-room. He paced the floor for a couple of minutes, then returned to the bedroom, unstrapped his Gladstone, pawed around under the clothes until his hand encountered cold steel. He lifted out a .45 automatic and stuffed it under his belt in a lightning gesture, buttoned his coat over it just as Phyllis looked up from unpacking a hatbox.

"Are you looking for your cognac bottle?" she asked.

Shayne said, "Yeh. My cognac bottle." He probed for the bottle and found it, went into the bathroom with it dangling from his fingers.

He set the bottle down and swiftly checked his automatic. It was loaded and the safety catch was on. He thrust it back under his belt, poured a small drink in a water glass, and went back into the room sipping it.

Phyllis smiled at him and said, "You run along and solve the case while I amuse myself in this gorgeous place pretending I'm the mistress of a retired hog raiser from Iowa."

Shayne set his empty glass down. "Okay. I'll let you know how things work out, Mrs. Shayne." He went out the door and closed it firmly behind him and sauntered down the hall to 312.

The door was closed but dim light showed through the transom. Shayne's eyes were bleak as he stopped in front of the door. He slid his hand down to the butt of his weapon and pushed off the safety. He knocked once and then twice, standing crouched and tense.

The door opened instantly and silently.

Shayne's lunge smashed the door back against the man

who was opening it. His own body force carried him past the descending blackjack in the hand of the other man ambushed against the threshold.

Checking his rush, he whirled, pulling his gun free and dropping to his knees as the man beside the open door dropped his blackjack and cursed gutturally, dragging a pistol from a shoulder holster.

Shayne shot him through his thick neck as the gun came out, then drove another slug into his open-mouthed surprise as he toppled forward.

Pain stung Shayne's belly muscles like a searing flame. He lurched sideways and snapped a bullet at the youth who had been flung back when the door crashed and now held a smoking revolver in his hand.

A nickeled .32 thudded to the rug and the pallid-faced lad went slowly to his knees, both hands hugging his stomach. A low whimper escaped his lips as he crouched there. His eyes glazed slowly and he went limp to the floor. His legs twitched and gray slobber drooled from between bloodless lips.

Shayne sat crosslegged on the rug and dropped his pistol in front of him. He put his hand to his side and it came away smeared with blood. Then he investigated more carefully and sighed with relief. It was only a flesh wound, nicking the muscles between rib-ends and hipbone.

He got to his feet wearily when people began to come into the room through the open door.

He grinned and waggled his finger at Phyllis when he saw her pushing in behind the others. Above the excited chattering and questioning and hysterical pandemonium he pantomimed to her that he could do with a drink, then moved back to sit upon the bed when she nodded and her pale, frightened face disappeared.

Chapter Three: FRONT-PAGE NEWS

THE TROPICAL HOTEL HOUSE DETECTIVE and an assistant manager made quick work of clearing the room of ogling bellboys and hysterical guests.

The house detective was a fat man with rosy cheeks and a pleasant expression. His slightly bulging eyes were grave as he bent over first one body and then the other. He made mumbling noises to himself, but spoke no intelligible words aloud. When he stood up, his gaze swept around the room as if seeking to place proper blame upon whoever had entered his premises and disturbed the even tenor of his way.

The assistant manager was tall and twittery and somewhat distinguished by perfect attire and Oxford glasses which failed to remain astride his prominent nose in coordination with his nervous gestures. He stood in the center of the room, plainly dismayed, yet apparently determined to reveal himself as an official of the hotel.

"This sort of thing is appalling, dreadfully appalling," he said finally to Shayne. He caught his glasses in midair and settled them firmly on his nose. "We have the hotel's reputation to think of."

The entrance of a physician through the open door cut short further reproval by the assistant manager. Behind him, Phyllis appeared with her hands behind her. All eyes were on the doctor as he bent over the bodies with a stethoscope which he took from his hip pocket, and no one paid any attention to Phyllis as she crossed the room to sit beside her husband on the bed. Her eyes were still dilated with fright and her face white, but her fingers were steady when she pulled the cork.

Shayne took a long drink and grinned at her. He said, "Thanks, angel," and winced as he inadvertently moved the injured portion of his body.

Watching him narrowly, Phyllis caught her breath at the sight of blood on the spread between them. She sprang to her feet and cried out to the doctor:

"My husband— Doctor, he's injured. He is bleeding to death. Do something!"

The doctor looked up mildly into her dark agitated eyes, folded the stethoscope tenderly, and returned it to his hip pocket. "I can't do anything for these men," he said. "They're dead." He stood up and went to Shayne. "What happened to you? Did you stop a bullet too?"

"Here," Shayne said, indicating the spot. He lay back across the bed with his hand holding the wound.

The doctor deftly disinfected and bandaged the wound while Phyllis looked on in an agony of terror. Suddenly she ran from the room and returned with a clean undershirt and a fresh shirt. The doctor smiled gravely at her pale face when Shayne growled:

"There's no time for that."

"But, Michael, you're all blood," she cried.

"You can change suits later," the doctor told him amiably, and assisted Phyllis in disrobing Shayne's torso and getting him into a clean undershirt.

Shayne did not resist them until his gray eyes strayed to the door as two men entered. "Damn," he muttered, and grabbed the top shirt and put it on unassisted.

One of the men was a burly fellow with a black felt pushed far back on his forehead. A silver star sagged from his open coat and the word *Chief* was engraved on it. He wore a movie-cowboy cartridge belt with a .45 swinging rakishly low in an open holster. He heeled the door shut and spoke harshly and authoritatively to the hotel detective:

"What's going on here, Gleason?"

Before Gleason could reply, the little man who entered with the chief chuckled happily and said:

"It looks like big city methods have come to Cocopalm, Chief Boyle. This is Michael Shayne or I miss my guess." He jerked a bushy, oversized head toward the tall detective sitting on the edge of the bed.

"Shayne? Damned if I like this." Chief Boyle thrust a belligerent, double-chinned jaw toward Shayne.

"I don't care a hell of a lot for it myself," Shayne drawled.

Phyllis stood by patiently holding his necktie in her hand. He reached up and took it from her, saying under his breath, "Go on back to your room, angel. This is no place for you."

Her eyes flashed defiance. She didn't say anything, but stepped back into a corner and sank into a deep chair, her eyes very bright and angry on Chief Boyle, who scowled down at Shayne's automatic lying on the floor.

He asked, "Is this your gun, Shayne?"

Shayne said, "Yes. I've got a permit to carry it."

"But no permit to go around killing people." The chief frowned. "I've heard about the rough stuff you pull in Miami, but it won't go here in Cocopalm."

The little whiplash of a man chuckled fiendishly behind the chief. "You've plugged a pair of our most reputable citizens," he said with sharp irony. "I figured you'd give us action, Shayne, but I wasn't expecting it so soon."

"Neither was I," Shayne retorted. He whipped the necktie around his collar and let it hang. "Are you Hardeman?"

"Good Lord, no. I'm Gil Matrix, editor, owner and publisher of the *Voice*. Prints all the news that's fit to print and a lot that isn't. Let me be the first to welcome you to our city." Matrix pushed forward and held out his hand.

Shayne took it, grunting sourly, "I've already been met by a reception committee that can probably be traced to the front-page stuff you ran this afternoon."

Matrix's grin was unabashed. "I meant to stir things up. Lord," he muttered, his eyes going again to the dead figures on the floor, "and did I ever! Chief Boyle here has been sitting on the lid too long and it was time the powder keg exploded."

"That'll be enough from you, Gil." Chief Boyle stepped angrily into the center of the room, shouldering the undersized editor aside with his great bulk. He glared down at Shayne, who now nonchalantly tied his tie. "What have you done with Mr. Hardeman?"

Shayne shot him a quick curious glance. "Hell, I haven't got him." He got up slowly and nodded toward the two dead men. "I thought one of those was Hardeman."

Boyle's eyes were hot with incredulity and disbelief as he stepped back a pace. "You thought one of *them* was—"

"On my right lies Pug Leroy," Gil Matrix said in a loud voice, his hands thrust deep in his trouser pockets as he circled the thick-bodied man on the floor. He shrugged heavy, slightly hunched shoulders which made his short body seem incongruous.

"Leroy," he went on dramatically, "has been working toward murder through the gentler stages of crime for a couple of years. His demise won't be excessively mourned.

"And this other lad is Bud Taylor, a local product." He spoke in a harsh, rasping voice, looking down at the thin-faced, youthful gunman who could not have been more than twenty-two.

There was utter silence in the room.

The little man dominated the scene as his owlishly round eyes slowly challenged everyone in the room, beginning with Chief Boyle, who was standing to one side with the hotel detective, passing on to the subdued assistant manager, and finally stopping when they rested upon Phyllis, who shrank deeper into her chair. The doctor, whose back was turned, silently closed his medical bag and stole from the room.

"Bud Taylor," Gil Matrix repeated, "one of those unfortunate weaklings easily led astray—a product of his environment, let us say. A youth who could have taken the right turn, but was induced to take the wrong one. We are all responsible for the Bud Taylors of this world," he went on fiercely. "Every one of us ensconced in our citadels of smugness who tolerate a festering growth in our community that sucks in a lad like Bud Taylor with the glamour of easy money. Easy money," he repeated in a strange whisper. "We shall all be judged," he jerked out, "I say—"

"Cut out the oration, Gil." Chief Boyle produced a handkerchief and mopped his sweating face. "This ain't the time or the place for a sermon."

"There'll be no better time or place," Matrix told him wrathly. "You ought to be down on your knees asking God to pity the citizens of Cocopalm who entrust their security to your supine hands—"

"Maybe the parson'll let you preach the funeral sermon," Chief Boyle snapped angrily.

The interruption left Matrix undismayed. His round eyes were bleak as he waved a hand and continued: "So long as you allow the Rendezvous to flourish under police protection on the outskirts of Cocopalm, just so long will we have the spectacle of our youth turning into gangsters and gunmen—and *worse*."

"Now see here, Gil," Boyle roared, "you know damn well the Rendezvous is out of the city limits and out of my jurisdiction."

"Yes, and I also know that Grant MacFarlane is your brother-in-law," Matrix lashed back. "You can't deny that Bud Taylor has been hanging around out there getting himself inoculated with the idea that the law is something to beat, to be scoffed at—which, by God, it is here in Cocopalm—and that he—"

"Shut up, Gil." Chief Boyle's voice was loud with authority. His face was the color of raw beef.

Shayne's amusement at the scene was wearing thin. He came impatiently to his feet and said, "I'm inclined to agree with the chief. I'd like to get your ideas later, Matrix, but right now I'm wondering why Mr. Hardeman wasn't here in this room to keep his appointment with me. While you fellows are throwing the gab around he might be needing help."

The assistant manager came to life, shook his head vigorously, and deftly caught his big-rimmed Oxford glasses as they flew from his nose. He readjusted them and glanced around the room with officious, but nevertheless nervous eyes. "Mr. Hardeman doesn't seem to be here at all. I happen to know that his engagement with Mr. Shayne was important. He gave orders that the detective was to be shown up immediately, and I'm quite positive he hasn't gone out since dinner."

Shayne's keen gray eyes traveled around the room to notice that three doors led away from the large bedroom.

One, in a corner behind the bed, stood slightly ajar, while another, across the room, was tightly closed as was the one leading to the hall. He saw, also, that Phyllis sat drawn back in her chair, her big dark eyes filled with questioning and wonderment. He shook his head at her and motioned toward the front door. Phyllis moved her own dark head slightly and negatively. Her soft round chin was set.

Shayne frowned and turned his attention to the two other doors. He strode to the closed one and jerked it open. It led into an empty tiled bathroom. His brows came down in a puzzled frown. Then he whirled about and went to the other door in the corner.

Jerking it open, he peered inside, then stepped back with a wide gesture. He said calmly:

"Come and see if this is Hardeman."

Matrix's nose quivered. He was the first to reach Shayne's side while the others crowded up.

"That's John Hardeman, all right," he chortled, "neatly done up in a knot."

Shayne looked steadily down at Hardeman for a moment and then stepped back, drawing the editor with him. Chief Boyle and Gleason dragged the bound and gagged race-track manager out of the spacious closet.

His body was long, big boned and heavy shouldered, but not fleshy. His forehead was of the high sort that is popularly supposed to be intellectual. His face was deeply suntanned, and his hair and eyes were gray. At the moment, indeed, his eyes rolled upward and around the room wildly. Gleason bent over him and struggled with the knot of the handkerchief at the back of his head; Chief Boyle took out his knife and cut the cords binding his arms.

Hardeman came slowly to his feet, sputtering incoherently and spitting a wad of cotton from his mouth. "This is ghastly," he complained, "a ghastly experience, to lie helpless in the closet and hear two assailants cold-bloodedly plan Shayne's murder. I must say you handled the situation masterfully."

He seized Shayne's hand in a bone-numbing grip and shook it. "I was terrified when I heard the telephone ring and one of them answer it. Pug Leroy it was. He simulated my voice almost perfectly. Those were moments of sheer agony when I listened to them take their places beside the door and wait to hear you knock." He paused to pluck a small piece of cotton from his tongue. Shayne wondered if that accounted for the high-flown manner in which he spoke and concluded that it didn't. "When the shooting began I couldn't conceive how you might escape with your life. If they had succeeded in killing you, I would certainly have been next."

"It's lucky for you they left the door open a crack so you wouldn't smother," Shayne interposed gravely when the man stopped for a long-drawn breath.

"You can't imagine my relief," Hardeman continued, "when I heard the others enter the room and I gathered that you had actually turned the tables on those murderous rogues. I must confess, though, no one seemed unduly curious as to my whereabouts," he ended with a reproachful glance at the men standing around the room.

"Did the thugs do any talking that made sense?" Shayne demanded. "Could you gather who or what was behind the attack on me?"

"Very little." Hardeman pursed his lips, spat out another small piece of cotton, then shook his head. He whipped out a handkerchief and mopped his forehead. "They assured me that I would not be harmed if they succeeded in their designs on you. I didn't put any trust in their promise. The motivation behind the attack was evidently your appearance here in Cocopalm to investigate the counterfeit racing-tickets."

"It seems a reasonable assumption," Shayne conceded dryly. "And I think I can thank our crusader editor for arranging things so neatly in my behalf. His front-page story was an invitation for something like this."

"Don't thank me," Matrix protested with a thin smile. "It was printed as a public service. Hardeman has been reluctant to take the bull by the horns and call in outside help, and I forced his hand by making you front-page news after he agreed to ask for your help."

"And making it impossible for me to get any line on who was behind the attack," Shayne pointed out harshly. "Instead of having those directly interested know I was coming, you made it common knowledge."

"I certainly had no intention of broadcasting it," Hardeman avowed. He shot a malevolent glance at the editor. "I might even suggest that Matrix hoped for some such result when he printed the story."

"You've got to admit it worked, if that *was* what I wanted," Matrix chortled. "This little affair is going to sell a lot of papers tomorrow."

Shayne turned away from him with a grunt of disgust. "Let's go to my room for our conference, Mr. Hardeman." He stooped to pick up his automatic, which still lay on the floor, but Chief Boyle stopped him.

"Better let me have that gun. I'm not rightly sure but what I ought to lock you up to boot."

Shayne straightened up with the weapon dangling from his fingers. "I told you I had a permit to carry it."

"There's been killing done," the chief persisted doggedly. "Don't you go trying to push me around like you push the cops in Miami. Inciting trouble, that's what you're doing, coming in here and stirring things up."

Shayne snorted and thrust the gun in his belt. He turned to Hardeman and asked curtly, "Are you coming?"

"See here, now," the chief began, but Shayne strode past him to Phyllis, who held out both her hands as if she doubted her strength to stand alone. He lifted her from the chair and held her firmly by the arm, steering her from the room.

Hardeman followed after a moment's hesitation, and Matrix edged past Boyle, chuckling maliciously. "You'd better call up Grant MacFarlane for further orders. He's likely to be very unhappy about all this."

At the door of their suite Shayne stood aside while Phyllis and Hardeman passed through. Gil Matrix came up behind them and aggressively caught the door knob as Shayne started to close the door.

"You'd better let me sit in on this conference, Shayne," he warned. "The *Voice* prints all the news and we have to guess at what we don't know. If you want factual reporting, don't shut me out."

Shayne stared speculatively at the little man, then nodded and allowed Matrix to enter.

Chapter Four: THE PRESSURE IS ON

PHYLLIS HAD GONE UNOBTRUSIVELY INTO THE BEDROOM and closed the door when Shayne entered behind Matrix. Hardeman was mopping his brow again. When he saw the editor, he asked his host fretfully:

"Need we make this a public meeting? It seems to me our business could be much better discussed in private."

Shayne ignored his question and motioned both men to be seated. "I like to get all the angles on a new case. I presume," he turned to Matrix, "you have some ideas regarding this counterfeiting proposition."

Matrix laughed harshly and perched himself on the arm of a chair. "Any man with one eye and the brain of a gnat would have an idea. Hell, who do you think turned those two punks on you in Hardeman's room?"

"I don't know," Shayne replied mildly. "My only thought is that your newspaper story set the thing up for them."

"All right. Maybe it did." Matrix spread out thin fingers and closed them into a tight fist. "It brought matters to a head. Things that have been simmering and stinking beneath the surface too long. Grant MacFarlane knew the jig was up when I finally prodded Hardeman into calling you in. He knows your reputation and he knew he had to take quick action. That reception in Hardeman's room was his answer to the threat."

Shayne asked, "Are you accusing this MacFarlane of doing the counterfeiting?"

The fiery little editor hesitated briefly, then nodded vigorously. "He's your best bet. His Rendezvous is nothing but a hangout for hoodlums from all the way up and down the coast. It would take quite an organization to cash all the forged tickets that have been going through the payoff windows lately."

"Is that the only evidence you have against him—the fact that you don't like him and that he has facilities for running such a deal?"

"Exactly what I've said to Matrix time and again," Hardeman complained. "He keeps insisting that we should force Chief Boyle to take some action against MacFarlane, while I contend that Boyle is a thoroughly honest though somewhat bewildered officer of the law."

"Boyle is under MacFarlane's thumb," Matrix barked. "You can't laugh that off."

"I invited you in here to get the news," Shayne reminded Matrix. "There won't be any news if you don't let me find out some things from Hardeman."

"There never is any news in this damn burg anyway," Matrix grated viciously. "I have to *make* a headline if any are printed. Which reminds me"—he jumped to his feet excitedly—"I should be getting some pix of those bodies before Boyle has them removed." He scurried out unceremoniously and slammed the door.

"You mustn't mind Matrix too much," Hardeman said stiffly. "Like all little men, he is ferociously determined to overcome the unfair deal he feels nature gave him when he was created. He's quite a town character, really. Came here a few years ago a total stranger. He has built up the *Voice* from a struggling weekly into an aggressive and somewhat progressive daily."

Shayne nodded. "Let's get down to cases on this counterfeiting. How long has it been going on?"

"For weeks. Though we didn't actually know we were cashing counterfeit tickets until a few days ago."

"So?" Shayne's right eyebrow arched quizzically.

"We have been noting shortages for some time. Annoying and inexplicable," Hardeman went on, "but not large enough sums to cause any great concern. We have a totalizer at the track, you understand, and it is exceedingly difficult for a dishonest clerk to get away with any irregularities. We checked and double-checked quietly, and were thoroughly stumped for a time. We even had an expert up from Miami to go over the totalizer and he pronounced it in perfect condition. Yet each night's play found us actually losing money instead of earning the percentage provided by law."

John Hardeman paused to mop his forehead. He shook his gray head sadly and winced at the thought of the outrageous state of affairs in which race-track patrons were getting more than an even break. Then he resumed:

"There was only one possible answer. We were cashing more win tickets than we were selling. It was quickly established that this was a fact, but a careful examination of the cashed tickets failed to reveal the counterfeits. The forgeries are so cleverly done as actually to defy detection, even though we know a certain portion of them are counterfeits. You can see how impossible it would be for a paying teller to detect a counterfeit in the confusion of cashing tickets after each race. And there is no way to make a man identify himself as having actually purchased the ticket he presents for payment. If it isn't stopped at once, Mr. Shayne, the track will have to close down."

"How much is the take amounting to?"

Hardeman shuddered. "More than three thousand dollars last night. You can see how easily it runs into a stupendous amount when you consider that many of the tickets pay off as much as ten or fifteen to one. It wouldn't take many persons mixing with the honest patrons to cash in several thousand dollars in forgeries."

"Who prints the tickets?"

"They are printed right here in Cocopalm at a small shop just down the street. We called for bids at the beginning of the season and the Elite Printing Shop underbid Matrix, who has the only other printing establishment in town. The Elite, by the way, is owned by a reputable citizen, a brother of one of our largest stockholders—a circumstance which Matrix chose to believe had a bearing on the awarding of the contract, but such was not the case."

Shayne frowned and rubbed his angular chin. "Seems to me you might try making an identifying mark on each genuine ticket as it is sold. In that way you could catch the counterfeit as it is presented."

"We thought of that almost at once," Hardeman answered. "The counterfeits came through just the same, marked exactly like the others. We inferred that the crooks were taking the simple precaution of buying a ticket on each race to guard against just such a ruse."

Shayne nodded glumly. "I guess it wasn't such a smart idea."

Conversation languished for a few minutes while both men sat in deep thought, then Shayne said, "It seems to me you could change the design of the tickets from day to day—vary the wording or the type used. Change the shape or color of the tickets."

The suggestion appeared to bore Mr. Hardeman. He said wearily, "We did not call in an outside detective until we had tried all such obvious remedies and found them worthless, Mr. Shayne. The counterfeiter uses his brains. Though we varied the tickets from one night to the next the forgeries turned up just the same, always exact duplicates of the new set for that night."

Shayne stood up and took a few paces around the room, tugging at his earlobe, then disappeared into the bathroom. He came back with a bottle and two glasses. "Have a drink," he offered.

Hardeman declined with thanks. Shayne poured a water glass half full. "I think better with a drink inside of me." He sat down, nursing the glass in his big palm.

"From what you say," he resumed, "I judge this is an inside job. Someone who knows what the new design is going to be must tip off the counterfeiters."

"That deduction is obvious," John Hardeman agreed dryly. "Though we have taken every precaution to keep each new batch a secret until we begin selling them at the track."

"There is evidently some precaution which you haven't taken," Shayne argued. "Who decides on the new design?"

"I— and I alone. No one else knows what the tickets will look like until I go to the Elite Printing Shop just in time to have them set up and run off before the races. Mr. Payson, one of the largest stockholders and the brother of the printer, accompanies me to the shop and he or I manage to remain constantly on guard while the type is set up and the printing done. As the tickets are finished, Chief Boyle takes charge of them and sees to their delivery at the track just in time for distribution to the selling windows. I tell you, Shayne, it isn't possible—yet forgeries are ready at the end of the first race."

"How many employees at the print shop see the tickets?"

"Only two in addition to the proprietor. Both are men above reproach, and they have been kept under close surveillance from the time the tickets are printed until the races start."

"But someone tips off the counterfeiters in time for them to get their tickets printed," Shayne argued.

"That's quite true." Hardeman made a hopeless gesture. "It is your problem now, Mr. Shayne."

"How about my fee?"

John Hardeman took a folded paper from his pocket

and handed it to Shayne. "At a board meeting last night it was agreed that your fee should be in direct proportion to the time it takes you to produce results. In other words, the sooner the counterfeiters are stopped, the more money the track will save. We agreed to give you a week. Continuing as we are now, the track stands to lose at least twenty thousand dollars during that week. We will pay you whatever portion of that twenty thousand you save us."

Shayne read the document and put it in his inside coat pocket. "The agreement seems all right. And—I get nothing if I don't get results within the week?"

"That's right. We plan to close down the track if you fail."

Shayne finished off his drink, grinned, and stretching his long legs out in front of him, sat contemplating the toes of his number twelves. "That puts the pressure on me to get started. I like that. Let me check, now. The newspaper office is the only other printing plant in town?"

"That's correct. The *Voice* office is right across the street, on the second floor. There are only three vacant lots between it and the Elite, a job printing plant. There are no intervening buildings."

Shayne looked up quickly as a harsh note crept into Hardeman's voice. "Do you suspect Matrix?" he asked pointedly.

"Please, Mr. Shayne, I suspect no one in particular. I simply state facts." Hardeman spoke impatiently.

Shayne nodded. "Okay. I think I've got the picture clear in my mind." He paused to light a cigarette, puffed smoke through his nostrils, and asked, "How well do you know Mayme Martin?"

Hardeman's thin smile showed mild surprise. "Not very well. She is a common figure around Cocopalm—turned up here soon after Matrix arrived. Until a few months ago she occupied an adjoining apartment to Matrix's. It was common gossip that—ah—the connecting door was not always kept locked," he ended delicately with a glance toward the bedroom door of Shayne's suite.

Shayne followed his glance and saw that the door had been opened a crack. He said, "You mean Miss Martin and Matrix were living together?"

Hardeman lifted his shoulders and spread out his long fingers. "Matrix is a bachelor, or represents himself to be one. I believe he doesn't deny that he and Miss Martin were acquainted before they came to Cocopalm."

"And now they're busted up?" Shayne persisted.

"I couldn't vouch for that. She moved from the apartment a few months ago and hasn't been seen much with him in public since. Why do you ask?" he ended curiously.

"I had a talk with the woman in Miami this afternoon." Shayne paused, rubbed his chin, then stood up. "I think my next move is a talk with Grant MacFarlane."

"I'd be careful in approaching him. He has a reputation for ruthlessness."

Shayne said, "So have I," with a wolfish grin. "There's one other thing," he continued as Hardeman stood up. "You heard Matrix say tonight that he felt it was necessary to publish that item about me in order to force you to go through with the idea of calling me in. Yet you say the board of directors actually made that decision last night. If that's true, Matrix must have known no forcing was needed."

"Certainly he knew it. He simply wanted to create a sensation, and when it backfired into an attempt on your life, he gave the only excuse he could think of."

Shayne's eyes glinted. "I see. That's a point I'll take up

with Matrix direct. Now, I presume I'm keeping you from the track."

"Yes. I should have been in my office before this."

Shayne went to the door and opened it. "I'll get right to work," he promised. "I'll let you know as soon as I begin to get results."

"Don't hesitate to call on me for any information I can supply," Hardeman requested as he turned and went down the hall.

Shayne closed the door and turned to see Phyllis flying noiselessly across the deep carpet. "There, now," she exclaimed ecstatically, "aren't you glad I'm such an efficient secretary? Twenty thousand dollars!"

"I haven't earned it yet, angel."

"But you will. Oh—I almost forgot—how is your side?" She caught his arm and urged him toward the bedroom.

"It's not bad," he declared. "A bullet picks on a tough customer when it whizzes in my direction." He grinned reassuringly. "Of course, a little drink—"

"I know. Your brain cells need stimulating, but you're not going to have a drop until you change suits." She got behind him and shoved him into the bedroom. "Blood is all caked on that one."

When he started undressing she went back to the living-room and picked up his glass, took it to the bathroom for a refill. She returned sober-faced and anxious. "Promise you'll be more careful, Michael. Everything depends on where a bullet hits."

Shayne buckled the belt of a fresh pair of trousers and said casually, "There's no danger now. This case looks too open and shut. I'm afraid of it—but I think the hoodlums will lay off of me from now on."

"You suspect Mr. Matrix, don't you? Everybody else

does." Shayne put on his coat and she followed him into the living-room, where he sank into a chair and set his glass on a table near by.

"I always begin a case by suspecting everybody," he said.

She snuggled down beside him in the big chair. "Don't you think Mr. Hardeman suspects the editor?" she persisted.

Shayne rumpled up his forehead and answered, "Hardeman hates Matrix," absently. He took a long sip of cognac and started across the room.

"What did you mean by asking about Mayme Martin?"

"Just wanted to find out. Miss Martin offered to crack the case for a grand, and I put her off. I might have made twenty grand by betting one that she was telling the truth."

Phyllis caught her lower lip between perfect white teeth, her big dark eyes round and thoughtful. Thinking made her look extremely young—younger than her twenty years. She said, "The chances are Mayme Martin knows a lot if she has been Mr. Matrix's mistress. If *I* were anyone's mistress, I'd not hesitate to listen in at a keyhole."

Shayne chuckled. His steel-gray eyes softened upon his young wife. "Mayme may be on the level," he said, then resumed his vacant stare across the room. He cracked his knuckles audibly.

"Every day that passes while you're solving the case costs you three thousand dollars," Phyllis reminded him sweetly.

"All women are mercenary," Shayne grinned. He sobered immediately and added, "A thousand bucks paid to Mayme Martin would net me two if her information would save me a day." He eased her head from his shoulder and stood up. "Let's go for a ride, angel."

"To Miami—to see Miss Martin?"

Shayne nodded. "We can make it there and back in an hour. We won't be missed from Cocopalm. No one needs to know we've gone."

He waited impatiently while she got a fur chubby from the closet and slipped into it. He jammed a hat down on his head and they went through the hall together.

Chief Boyle stepped from the open door of Hardeman's room to intercept them.

Shayne's fingers tightened on his wife's arm. He stopped in front of the chief and asked curtly, "What's on your mind now?"

Boyle stood his ground, glowering, a pugnacious jaw outthrust. "Where are you going?"

Shayne said, "Out."

"I can't have a man just walk in here and shoot up the town, kill two men, without holding him responsible," the chief protested. He frowned weightily.

Shayne smiled. "Are you going to arrest me for being an old meanie and not standing around with my hands in my pockets while your brother-in-law's thugs blast my guts out?"

"I'm not saying the shooting wasn't justified," the chief admitted gravely. "But that's something a coroner's jury will have to decide. I'll have to ask you not to leave town until after the inquest tomorrow."

Shayne said, "All right, you've asked me." He steered Phyllis forward. The chief backed away a step but did not move aside.

"Not so fast there. You haven't said you'd stay."

Shayne's lips curled away from his teeth. He put Phyllis gently aside, but she clung to his arm, her face white with strain.

"Don't dive in over your depth," Shayne warned Boyle. "I'll smash any man who stands in my way tonight." His big hands balled into fists. He shifted his weight to a fighter's stance.

Phyllis breathed, "Please, Michael," and tugged at his hard arm. She appealed to the chief, "Don't be absurd. My husband isn't going to run away from any inquest. He has a job to do, and—"

"Don't make it easy on him," Shayne said angrily. "I'm not asking his permission to do anything."

"Well, now," Boyle said placatingly, "if the lady gives me her word I guess that's good enough. You folks go ahead, but I can't guarantee to give you protection if you don't tell me what you're going to do."

Shayne snorted and strode past him with his wife clinging to his arm. She smiled up into his sultry eyes as he stalked to the elevator.

"Why do you insist on being so tactless, Michael?" she asked with a catch in her voice. "You could avoid all sorts of complications if you would just leave a man like that a little corner to back into. He's sort of pathetic," she ended thoughtfully.

Shayne laughed suddenly and in a wondering tone said, "You're marvelous, Phyl. I'll never understand how I got along all these years without you." He squeezed her arm with rough tenderness, then lifted her into the elevator as it stopped in front of them.

Chapter Five: THE SMELL OF BLOOD

THE SKY WAS CLEAR AND DUSKILY BLUE from the pale light of a quarter moon when they got into the roadster. There was little traffic going south, and in spite of the parade of racing cars traveling north toward the race track, Shayne reached the outskirts of Miami in thirty minutes. He glanced at his watch as he slowed for the traffic signal at 79th Street, then swerved to the right off the boulevard.

He said, "I've got to find some place where I can get a check cashed, angel," in response to a silent inquiry in her dark eyes. "The Lucky-Seven Club will just about be opening for business and that's my best bet to pick up a thousand dollars at this hour."

They bumped across the F.E.C. tracks at Little River, turned left on Northeast Second Avenue. A dozen blocks farther south he turned into a graveled circle drive leading through tropical shrubbery to the front of a solid stucco structure set unobtrusively back from the street. The neon light was not on over the entrance, but curtained windows glowed with lights from within.

Shayne stopped in front of the door and got out. "I'll only be a minute," he promised, striding around the car and up flagstone steps.

He put his finger on the electric button and held it down. After a few seconds a bulb glowed above his head and a panel in the door slid back. A pair of black eyes set in white orbs rolled at him through the slit, then the latch clicked and the door came open.

Shayne said, "Hello, Foots," to a fat Negro and received a nod and a white-toothed grin.

"You-all's moughty early tonight, Mistah Shayne. Ain't hahdly got the tables unkivered."

"Is Chips in his office?"

"Yassuh, he sho is. Mistah O'Neil am busy right now layin' out de money fo' tonight's play."

Shayne went down a carpeted hall past an archway opening into a huge square room where men were taking covers from roulette tables, crap layouts, and curved black-jack set-ups. He went through an open door and at the end of the hall said, "Hi, Chips," to a tall black-haired man who squatted on the floor in front of a large safe.

Chips O'Neil turned his head and said, "Hello there, shamus." He stood up with neat bundles of bills in his hands, arching iron-gray eyebrows ironically. He complained, "Don't tell me I've got to start paying off the private dicks along with the regulars."

Shayne grinned. "This isn't a jerkdown—unless my check bounces." He took a checkbook from his pocket and sat down at a desk. "Can you let me have a grand?"

"Sure. How do you want it?"

"Make it twenties." He made out a check to *Cash* and signed it.

"A ransom payoff?" O'Neil asked curiously as he counted out a stack of twenties.

Shayne smoothed the bills and folded them into a wallet. "Nothing like that. Just a little matter of business. Thanks, Chips."

Chips O'Neil said, "That's okay, shamus," and Shayne went out to his car. He nodded to Phyllis as he stepped on the starter. "I got the money. When I spread this stuff out in front of Mayme Martin she'll tell me everything she knows."

He drove on down Second Avenue and parked opposite the Red Rose Apartments. When Phyllis started to unlatch the door on her side, he said, "Better stay in the car, angel."

"But I want to come in," she protested. "Why are you always trying to make me stay back or get out of the room when something interesting is about to happen?"

"In this case, because I'd hate to have anyone see me

taking you in there. They might get the wrong idea. This dump," he went on, jerking his head toward the flashy front lights of the building, "is what the *Herald* would chastely describe as a house of ill fame. After all, Phyl— unless you want to lose your reputation—"

"Oh!" Phyllis sank back against the cushion. "Why don't people tell me these things?"

"Because you're so sweet and innocent." Shayne pinched her cheek and got out. "Mayme may still be so polluted she won't be able to talk coherently. In that case I'll be right back."

He went across the street and into the entrance hall. Curtains were drawn across the brightly lighted lounging-room and loud voices and laughter followed him up the stairs to No. 14. The door was closed and no light showed through the transom.

He hesitated a moment with his knuckles doubled to knock, then tried the knob instead. The door opened easily.

A musty odor, part gin and part human, struck him in the face. Mingled with it was a stale smell of indefinable sweetishness which caused the hairs at the back of his neck to prickle. He fumbled for the light switch, found it, but stepped back to close the door before turning on the lights.

Light flooded a disordered room which was occupied only by himself. He stood back against the door while his eyes searched every nook and corner for the thing he expected to see.

It wasn't there. He went forward warily, glanced into the empty kitchenette, then went to the closed bathroom door. He hesitated for a moment, standing back from a little pool of blood that had seeped under the door. His face hardened into grim, gaunt lines as he took out a handkerchief and covered the doorknob.

The sweetish smell of fresh human blood was strong when he opened the door. He found the bathroom light switch and snapped it on, stood staring somberly down at the corpse of Mayme Martin. Her body lay twisted on one side and there was something indecent in the sight of her naked legs below the hem of her slip.

He stood rigidly in the doorway and took in every detail of the scene with cold, searching eyes. Mayme Martin's throat was slit from ear to ear and the pool of blood on the floor was turning brown.

There was an odd look of contentment on her features, which had been so distorted with anger and fear a short time before. There was nothing to indicate that she had struggled while the lifeblood drained from her body. A safety razor blade lay on the tile floor beneath the unflexed fingers of her right hand.

Shayne left the light on and closed the bathroom door with his handkerchief-filled hand. He mopped sweat from his face and stood staring around the living-room. His toe struck an empty gin bottle on the floor and it rattled loudly against the leg of a chair as he moved slowly forward.

The hatbox which had been half packed on his previous visit was now empty and toilet articles and clothing were scattered over the floor as though thrown aside by someone hastily searching through them.

Shayne went to the door without touching anything. He used his handkerchief to rub the inside knob clean, scrubbed the electric switch, then turned out the light and stepped into the hall. Here he carefully removed his fingerprints from the outside knob. There was no use trying to preserve the fingerprints of whoever had entered the room before him. His own prints had obliterated them.

The doors of rooms along the hall were closed except the one at the head of the stairs where the redhead had accosted him in the afternoon. He dragged the brim of his hat low on the left side of his face, tucked his chin down, and went down the stairs. He bumped into a man coming through the front door and the fellow squared off with a surly curse, but Shayne brushed past him and out to his roadster.

"What happened?" Phyllis asked eagerly as he got under the steering-wheel. "Was Mayme's information worth coming for? Did she tell you anything important?"

Shayne moved his head shortly and negatively, then relaxed behind the wheel and shoved his hat back from his forehead.

A cry of dismay escaped Phyllis's lips when she saw his face. "What is it, Michael? What happened up there?"

"Mayme Martin isn't going to do any talking—ever," he said harshly. "She's dead."

"Oh—" Phyllis pressed her hand against her mouth.

"It looks like suicide on the surface," he went on slowly, "but I think it was fixed to appear that way."

"You mean—murder?"

He nodded and leaned forward to turn on the ignition. "We'd better get away from here in a hurry."

"But shouldn't you tell the police, Mike? It might be hours before anyone will find her."

"Mayme won't mind," he muttered.

"But, Michael! Just think—"

He said, "No," with savage intensity and swerved around a corner toward Biscayne Boulevard.

Phyllis shrank away from him and he drove fast, looking straight ahead.

"She's dead," he said after a time. "Nothing can change that. Can't you see the spot I'd be in if I reported it?"

"I suppose so. Still—no one could blame you."

He laughed shortly, swinging into the boulevard northward. "I'm damned glad Mayme Martin wasn't murdered on Peter Painter's side of the bay. Of course, I know Will Gentry wouldn't suspect me of murder. But he'd want the answers to a lot of questions—answers I can't give him right now. I wouldn't blame him for not believing me. My story sounds screwy as hell, and he knows I never tell anything if I think I can make a fee by keeping still. He'd have to hold me, Phyl, and in the meantime there's a job to be done in Cocopalm. We've got to get back there so fast no one will suspect we've been away—and sit tight until this thing is cleared up."

In a small voice Phyllis said, "All right," and subsided against him.

Shayne nosed the roadster into the mad racing parade going north toward the dog track and held it at seventy-five.

Chapter Six: A GOOD PLACE FOR SNOOPING

THE RACES HAD STARTED when they approached the track for the second time. Shayne slowed the car and grinned at Phyllis, who sat up straight and intent, cocking her dark head toward the racketing sound of the mechanical rabbit and the gleeful yelps of the hounds pursuing it around the oval track.

He asked, "Want to stop and take in a few races while I go on into town and do some checking up?"

Phyllis shook her head regretfully. "It's no fun to go alone. Maybe you'll be coming out later to watch for counterfeit tickets and I'll come with you."

"It's going to be lonesome at the hotel," he warned her. "I'll be too busy the next hour or so to have you trailing me."

"Oh, I expect to be ditched," she told him resignedly. "I'll grow old and gray sitting around waiting and wondering whether you'll come back under your own power or be carried in."

Shayne grunted something unintelligible as he pulled up in front of the hotel and his headlights picked up two men standing together at the curb. They were Gil Matrix and Chief Boyle.

As he leaned forward to turn off the ignition, Shayne murmured. "Don't let anything slip about our trip to Miami."

She made a wry face at him and they got out together.

The fiery little editor greeted Shayne by saying, "We were wondering where you had gone. Chief Boyle was getting nervous waiting for the next shooting to start."

"That ain't so," Chief Boyle said. "I just said to Matrix I reckoned you and your wife had gone out to the dogs."

"A good guess," Shayne assured him. He took Phyllis's arm and led her into the lobby. "Wait here," he said. "I'll be back to report presently."

He rejoined the two men at the curb and asked, "Where could I find Grant MacFarlane this time of night?"

Gil Matrix chuckled. "You'd better have your gun greased for a quick draw with MacFarlane. He's not going to like what happened to those two punks upstairs tonight."

"You shut up, Gil." Chief Boyle worried his underlip with his teeth. "You can't prove Leroy and Taylor were working for Grant tonight. They could've been hired by anybody that wanted Mr. Shayne out of the way. Grant can't help it if fellows like that hang around his night club."

"I reiterate," Matrix returned ironically, "Shayne had better be ready to duck more lead if he insists on looking MacFarlane up tonight."

Shayne said, "I haven't asked for advice. I just want to know where I can find the man."

"He'll be at the Rendezvous, just north of the city limits," Matrix informed him.

"But you better not go out there," Boyle interposed. "No need to stir up any more ruckus. Besides, I calculate it's my duty to see you don't go out of this city until there's a coroner's verdict on those two killings."

Shayne said, "The only way you can keep me away from the Rendezvous is by putting me in your jail."

"Well, now, maybe I'll do that." Boyle stepped back a pace, his eyes shifting away from Shayne's hard gaze.

The big detective laughed softly, his lips drawing back from his teeth. "It'll be one of the toughest pinches you ever made, Boyle."

"I don't want any trouble with you, Shayne," the big chief said. "But I guess I can round you up in case I want you." He turned and hurried down the street.

"You're what Cocopalm has been needing," Matrix said to Shayne as the chief passed out of sight. "There'll be more headlines after you and MacFarlane shoot it out."

Shayne warned, "You'll print one headline too many one of these days," but the editor only laughed and trotted across the street on his thin, short legs.

Shayne stood beside his car and watched Matrix with narrowed, speculative eyes.

A sign in a lighted second story window directly opposite blatantly proclaimed: *The Voice of Cocopalm*. North from the two-story building were the three vacant lots which Hardeman had described.

A tall, stoop-shouldered man passed in front of the lighted window as Shayne watched Matrix begin climbing a stairway leading up from the sidewalk. The man moved back into view as the editor entered the office. Shayne stood on the curb and watched them talking together. Matrix was gesticulating excitedly and the stoop-shouldered man kept nodding. Presently he took off a canvas apron that was tied around his waist and put on a hat and coat.

Shayne strolled across the street and intercepted the man as he came hurrying down the stairs. The detective deliberately lurched against him, grinned widely, and put a hand on his arm. "Hiya, pal. Lishen, I got shome newsh—"

"Not now." The man put him off impatiently. "Tell it to the editor upstairs."

Shayne sagged back against the building and hiccoughed gently. He watched while the *Voice* employee got into a Ford parked at the curb and drove southward to the intersection where he made a sweeping U turn and drove swiftly north. When he was out of sight, Shayne muttered, "H-m-m," and climbed the echoing wooden stairs. He pushed a door which opened into the lighted front office.

The office was small and untidy, with a littered desk, a steel filing-cabinet, and a typewriter stand in the corner. Matrix was not in the office, but an open door led back into a rear room through which light shone.

Shayne went to a north window and looked down across three vacant lots to the ground-floor Elite Printing Shop. He was standing at the window when he heard soft footsteps behind him. He turned slowly and saw Gil Matrix in the doorway regarding him with a twisted, unpleasant smile.

"What are you snooping around here for?"

"It's a good place for snooping," Shayne countered mildly. He turned away from the window and swung one leg over a corner of the editor's desk. Matrix entered with short, jerky steps, his shoulders hunched slightly forward. "I thought you were in an all-fired hurry to have it out with Grant MacFarlane," he said in a flat, grouchy tone.

Shayne moved his head slightly and negatively. He took a cigarette from a pack in his breast pocket, lit it, and flipped the match away. He grunted, "I didn't want to surprise him. You can never tell what fool thing a man will do when he is surprised and on the defensive. If I give him time to get ready for me the results will be more predictable—and fewer people are likely to get hurt."

"So that," Matrix mused, "is why you spouted off to Chief Boyle and told him where you were headed. I confess I thought it was a dumb trick—at the time. I was beginning to wonder whether you were as smart as you were rated."

Shayne smiled. "You think Boyle will warn MacFarlane I'm on my way out there?"

"I'm sure of it. One will get you a hundred that MacFarlane has already been told."

"I never bet against a sure thing." Shayne hesitated, drawing on his cigarette, his eyes slitted and inscrutable, then suddenly he asked, "What came between you and Mayme Martin a few months ago?"

Matrix swore softly and in complete surprise. His round eyes narrowed upon Shayne. "What do you know about Mayme Martin?"

"Not much. I understand you used to be quite intimate with her and broke off quite recently—and suddenly."

"So—that's where you were—getting acquainted with our pious psalmsingers here in Cocopalm," Matrix snarled. His strange eyes were full of venom. "Because Miss Martin and I were old friends and lived in adjoining apartments the lecherous-minded citizens added up two and two and immediately put us in bed together."

"Were you?" Shayne asked guilelessly.

"Why should I deny it? And why the inquisition? Are my morals involved in a counterfeiting case?"

"I don't know," Shayne answered truthfully. "I am interested in knowing why you broke off with Miss Martin."

"Because she got to sopping up more gin than was good for her. She was pickling her brains and her intestines with the stuff and she got sore when I told her she was beginning to look like an old hag—which she was."

"What happened to her after she moved away from next door to you?"

"She gravitated to the gutter," Matrix said bitterly. "Last time I saw her she was cadging drinks out at the Rendezvous and had a grudge against the world in general and me in particular. I'd still like to know where the hell she fits in."

Shayne sighed and carefully eased ashes from his cigarette onto the floor. "So would I." He cocked his ear to the sound of firm, authoritative steps climbing the echoing wooden stairway. "You're about to have another visitor," Shayne pronounced. An interested gleam came to his gray eyes.

Matrix nodded sourly. He jammed his hands deep into his pockets and paced the narrow confines of the office and back. He shouted, "Come," when the footsteps stopped outside and a knock sounded on the door.

A rotund, ruddy-featured man of medium height came in. He carried a stiff straw hat in his hand and had a rosy, perspiring bald head with a fringe of gray hair all the way around. He wore a Palm Beach suit with a gaudy shirt and gaudier tie. A round pot-bottom belly preceded him importantly into the newspaper office. He stopped, evidently abashed, and looked inquiringly at Shayne, then pursed his full pink lips and spoke in a rounded tone, "Ah—Mr. Matrix—I hoped to find you alone."

Matrix said, "Come on in, Mr. Payson. I've just been having a few words with the detective. Mr. Payson, this is Mr. Shayne, from Miami."

"The detective, eh?" Payson asked heartily. He followed his belly toward Shayne and held out a fat, perspiring palm. Shayne lounged to his feet and shook hands while Matrix explained:

"Mr. Payson is one of the largest stockholders of the dog track and chairman of the board. He has been having apoplexy since the counterfeiting, which accounts for his rosiness."

Payson said, "Ahem," with a deprecating sidelong glance at Matrix. "I'm glad to meet you, Mr. Shayne. We depend upon you, sir, to diagnose this unusual case. I may say that the entire community is depending upon you to take immediate and drastic steps. I need hardly point out what a calamity it would be to Cocopalm if the track were forced to shut its gates. It's one of our greatest tourist attractions, not to mention the hundreds of local families supported directly or indirectly by our payroll."

"And not forgetting the dividends—which have been sadly curtailed," Matrix put in with a sardonic grin.

Payson chuckled. "Ha ha. Amusing fellow, isn't he, Mr. Shayne? He flaunts a determined cynicism while actually he's one of our most aggressive civic boosters."

Shayne said, "If you want to talk privately to Mr. Matrix, I'll be going along." He dragged his big frame up from the desk.

"No, don't go," Matrix interposed. "Payson and I can talk in the back room. There's something else I want to take up with you before you go."

"Don't leave on my account," Payson concurred. "My business with Gil will take only a moment. I don't wish to slow the—er—wheels of justice, shall we say?"

He followed the editor through the door leading into the printing-shop and closed the door. Through the single wall Shayne could hear the older man talking at length in a low, guarded voice, but could distinguish no words.

At length Matrix said sharply and disagreeably, "All right, Payson, but it's against the principle that has made the *Voice* what it is. You know our slogan—all the news without fear or favor."

Payson's voice droned again placatingly, until Matrix interrupted, "I told you I would—let it go at that," and jerked the door open.

Payson came back into the office smiling in some constraint. He mumbled something to Shayne and went out the front door, closing it firmly behind him.

"The old goat," said Matrix viciously. "A pillar of the church, by God, and he practically controls the bank that holds my mortgage."

Shayne grinned at the dynamic little editor's vitriolic emphasis. "Suppressing a juicy bit of scandal?"

"Exactly. The old so-and-so has a good wife and two fine kids here in town, but he has evidently got himself tangled up with a wench in Miami. I was in Miami on business this afternoon and saw him on the street. Now he's in an uproar because I was going to print the news as a local item. Seems he told his wife he was making a business trip *up* the coast. If I had that mortgage paid off I'd print it whether or not. That's the sort of small-town stuff I'm running up against all the time here."

Shayne said, "This Payson—is he the brother of the proprietor of the other print shop in town?"

Matrix nodded and dropped into the chair before the desk. Shayne resumed his position, one hip on the corner of the littered desk.

"That relationship," Matrix continued, "cost me a nice juicy contract for printing the dog-track tickets last fall. I'm morally certain they opened my bid first, then arranged that the Elite bid a few dollars under my price."

Shayne said, "Hardeman told me that Payson and he divide the responsibility of getting the genuine tickets printed without a leak."

"That's right. If the old goat didn't own stock at the track I'd suspect him of having counterfeits printed."

"As it is," said Shayne casually, "how do you think the counterfeiters get hold of the new design each day in time to get their forgeries out? Hardeman claims that Boyle guards the printed tickets personally until they're delivered at the track."

"Humph. Who guards Boyle?" Matrix asked cynically. "That's the crux of the whole affair. Hardeman is just a trusting fool. He refuses to recognize the obvious fact that Boyle is only a tool for Grant MacFarlane."

"You hate MacFarlane?" Shayne asked softly.

"I don't deny it." Matrix glared at him, his thin face working. "I hate what MacFarlane stands for—the rottenness and filth our youth are taught to take for granted when they frequent a cesspool like the Rendezvous. Any man who preys on adolescents makes a business of warping immature minds and is the greatest menace in modern society."

Shayne nodded, swung himself to a standing position and said, "It's time I took a look-see at MacFarlane's sink of iniquity." He paused with his hand on the knob, half turned back into the room.

"You don't happen to know the name of Payson's light-of-love in Miami? Did you see him with her?"

"No, and he naturally didn't divulge any details."

Shayne said, "Naturally not. But if you have any way of finding out I'd like very much to know the lady's name."

He went through the door as Matrix stared after him in open-mouthed amazement.

Chapter Seven: SHE FORGOT HER ROLLER SKATES

SHAYNE CROSSED THE STREET TO HIS ROADSTER, still parked in front of the hotel. With his hand on the doorlatch, he hesitated and turned to look toward the entrance into the lobby where he had left Phyllis. Then he frowned, took a step forward, and stopped. Equally unaccountably, he grinned, turned back to the car, got in, backed away from the curb, and drove north through the business district of Cocopalm. Tall, clean-trunked royal palms lined the highway, their graceful fronds silvered with the pale light of a quarter moon.

Lounging back in the seat with his big hands loose on

the steering-wheel, Shayne drove slowly. He was waiting for something, he wasn't certain what. There was a subtle warning in the subdued murmur of the night breeze swaying silvery fronds along the way, in the gentle swish of combers on the shore to his right.

He nodded absently. It was best to leave Phyllis twiddling her thumbs in the hotel lobby.

The black macadam of the highway was strangely deserted, an unwavering path leading him onward between the slender white palm trunks which were like a double row of planted lances in the softly diffused light.

Headlights of an oncoming automobile cut a bright swath toward him. He slowed still more and watched it roar past. A Ford, and the driver was the stoop-shouldered man he had watched drive away from the *Voice* office.

When his headlights picked up the slender figure of the girl in the roadway ahead, Shayne felt no surprise. She was as much a part of the scene as the tall palms and the night silence. She was walking northward on the edge of the pavement, glancing back over her shoulder hopefully as he came up behind her.

She stopped suddenly and turned to face his headlights, not gesturing for a ride, but quite evidently offering herself for any adventure that might come. Few men would have passed her by on the lonely road, and certainly Michael Shayne was not one of those.

He braked the roadster to a stop beside her, seeing only that she was young and slender and held herself with an aloofness that was disconcertingly at variance with what one might reasonably expect of a roadside pickup.

The girl hesitated momentarily, then leaned forward on the door, putting her head and shoulders inside and looking at his face with grave, searching eyes. She had bright blond hair wound around her head in big braids with a tiny jaunty ribbon tucked on one side. Her breath came jerkily through parted lips that were too red.

Shayne decided that her eyes were blue. He grinned and asked, "Well, do I pass inspection?"

When she nodded without speaking he leaned over and released the door catch. "It doesn't cost any more to ride, and it's lots easier on shoe leather."

She nodded swiftly and slid in beside him, drawing a light silk cape protectingly about her shoulders and breast. She shivered and murmured with forced flippancy, "I forgot my roller skates."

Shayne reached past her and closed the door. He settled back and took out a pack of cigarettes, offered her one, but she shook her head; then, changing her mind, she reached for one. "I guess I will, too." Her voice was a deep-throated murmur.

Shayne held a match to the end of her cigarette and amusement came into his eyes as she puffed with bravado. She had a nice profile and a creamy soft complexion where there was not excessive rouge.

She said, "You're wondering—why I'm out here like this—walking down the road alone at night."

Shayne said, "Why, no. I was expecting you."

She jerked her bright head around quickly, lips parted in surprise. "You're crazy. You couldn't have been."

"All right," Shayne agreed, "I'm nuts. I guess it's the moon." He puffed on his cigarette serenely and waited for her to make the next move.

She fidgeted with her cape, holding it together with one hand while she held the cigarette in the other. "What I mean is," she said haltingly, "no one could have expected this to happen. Not even I. I thought Fred was a nice fellow." There was a note of deep injury in her throaty young voice.

"Wasn't he?" asked Shayne interestedly.

"I'll say he wasn't. He—well, a girl doesn't mind when she's stepping out to have a good time. But when he admitted he was married and had two kids—" She shrugged her slim shoulders and relapsed into gloomy silence.

"So your evening is completely spoiled?"

She gave him a long, demure glance out of the corner of her eye. "Does it have to be? What I mean is—we were headed out to the Rendezvous for a few drinks and dancing. I could certainly use a drink right now." She ended with a shaky, high-pitched laugh which the big detective did not believe originated in any gaiety on her part.

Shayne nodded gravely. He put the roadster in gear and let it snail forward. "How do you know I'm not married with a passel of brats at home?"

She smiled happily. "I can tell. You don't *look* married."

"Maybe Fred didn't either," he reminded her, "and not many girls would tumble to this old jalopy of mine."

She flashed him another quick, searching look, but Shayne's eyes were mild and he was smiling. "Well, you know how it is. I *did* hesitate to get in with you, but a girl gets bored stiff doing nothing night after night. I didn't think it would be any harm to go out to the Rendezvous with Fred tonight. My name," she tagged on as an afterthought, "is Midge."

Shayne inclined his head. "I'll answer to Mike—from you."

"You're nice," she breathed. "I can tell it already. You've got hair that makes a girl just itch to run her fingers through it. You're the kind who would know when a girl wants to be petted and when she wants to be let alone."

Shayne chuckled with genuine amusement. "I call this old jalopy of mine the Mayflower," he warned, "because so many puritans have come across in it."

Midge laughed delightedly and leaned back, pressing her silk-clad shoulder against him.

"I *thought* that gag was old enough to be new to a gal your age. Is that the Rendezvous ahead?" Shayne asked as they approached a building gleaming with red and yellow neon lights.

"That's it." She shivered and moved closer to him. "If you haven't ever been there before, drive around to the west entrance," she cajoled. "We can go in through a side door and upstairs to a private room where no one will see us."

"A private room? Are you ashamed of being seen with me?"

She laughed lightly. "Don't be silly." She trailed her knuckles over one of his big hands. "It's only—well, I can't afford to be seen at a place like the Rendezvous. My family —you know. Dad's a deacon in the church and he and mother would have a fit if they knew I'd ever taken a drink."

Shayne nodded and drove through an arched entrance, past rows of parked cars, and around to the west side of the rambling two-story building. A single green bulb burned over a closed oak door. Midge pointed it out. With a giggle that didn't quite ring true, she explained, "That's where all the high-school kids go in and out."

Shayne parked, got out, and she slid out after him. She caught his arm and held it tightly, pressing against him. The heavy door opened at the turn of the knob and they went into a long carpeted hallway. A burst of music came from beyond the partition, and there were loud voices and laughter.

Midge turned him to the right and led him to a stairway. "They gamble in the back upstairs," she told him in a conspiratorial whisper, "and they say you can order most anything you want served in the private rooms."

Shayne climbed the stairs with her and didn't probe further into the suggested evils of the upstairs rooms. A dark-featured man wearing a white mess jacket lounged at the top of the stairway. He nodded woodenly to Midge and led them to a closed door at the end of a row of closed doors. He opened it onto a dimly lit cubicle with a small table set for two. There was an overstuffed couch in the room and a deep club chair in the opposite corner. The man said, "I'll send a boy right up," and went out, closing the door behind him.

Shayne stood in the center of the small, intimately furnished room and rumpled his coarse hair. "It's a nice quiet place for high-school youngsters to do their consorting," he observed dryly. "Lots more fun learning the facts of life here than by observing bees and flowers."

Midge's laugh was constrained, as though she didn't quite know whether to take him seriously. She dropped onto the couch and took a compact from her purse, examined her face in the tiny mirror.

Shayne saw that she was older than she appeared in the moonlight and by the faint light on the instrument board. At least twenty-five. She was tall, and had extremely nice legs. The heels of her black suéde slippers were run down, and the backs of her hands showed clearly that they were used for hard work.

When a discreet knock sounded on the door, Shayne

swung around and opened it. A middle-aged waiter entered bearing a menu, but Shayne waved him aside. He asked the girl, "Would you like champagne?" and she clasped her hands to breathe, "Oh—yes."

"Domestic," Shayne ordered grimly. "Thirty-four or thirty-five—and bring me a triple slug of cognac in a beer mug. Martell, if you have it."

The waiter bowed and withdrew. Midge patted the couch beside her. "Sit here beside me. He'll pull a table up for us when he brings the drinks."

Shayne sat down, leaving a foot of space between them. He glanced past the table to a closed inner door and growled, "Where does that lead to?"

Midge followed his glance. Color crimsoned her cheeks. "I think that's a—a lavatory."

"You seem to know a hell of a lot about the setup," Shayne commented in a thoroughly disagreeable tone. "For a girl who knows her way around like you do, I can't quite feature you walking home from the buggy ride."

Her eyes lowered swiftly to her tightly clasped fingers. She drew her breath in with a little gasp and said sharply, "Just because I know about things is no reason for you to think I'm—bad."

Shayne laughed aloud at her naïve choice of the word. As yet he had no idea why he had been steered to the private room, but he was evidently going to have a few laughs finding out. He stopped laughing and assured Midge, "On the contrary, I think you're pretty damned nice."

He got up and wandered to the closed inner door, turned the knob without result. Midge watched him with eyes clearly frightened now. She murmured. "It's—I think it's connected with the next room too. They've locked it from the other side."

Shayne's eyes narrowed but he said nothing. He returned to sit beside the girl and called, "Come in," when a knock sounded on the outer door.

The waiter had a split of domestic champagne in a silver bucket of crushed ice, and a beer mug a third full of cognac on a tray. He deftly slid the table over in front of them, pulled the cork from the champagne bottle with a gratifying plop, then poured a tall glass of the cold bubbling liquid for Midge.

He laid a check face up before Shayne and waited stiffly. Shayne glanced at the total and whistled. The amount was $23.50—$15.00 was marked opposite the word *Service*.

Shayne shook his head angrily and pushed the bill aside. "That's highway robbery. I want to see the manager."

The waiter said, "It's perfectly correct, sir. The usual charge for a private room and allows you the use of it for as long as you wish it."

"To hell with that," Shayne growled in a murky tone of anger. "Send MacFarlane up here. I'll settle with him."

"Please—don't!" Midge grabbed his arm and raised terror-stricken blue eyes to his. "Don't make a scene. I— I couldn't stand it."

Shayne's laugh was harsh. "The old gag, eh? How many of his come-on gals has MacFarlane got lined up on the highway to lure suckers in for a fleecing? Hell," he went on with relaxed brutality, "I can rent a hotel room for a week with a woman thrown in for fifteen bucks."

Midge's hold on his arm grew lax. She shrank away from him, her face drained of color except for the red spots of rouge high on each cheek. "Don't say such things," she pleaded. "You don't really mean them."

"The hell I don't," Shayne jeered. He picked up the beer mug and drank half the cognac. "Get MacFarlane up here," he insisted to the waiter. "I'll tell him what I think of his gyp joint."

The waiter nodded and went out with a stiff bow.

Midge sank back, breathing in great piteous sobs. "I don't know what I'll do," she moaned. "Oh, how could you be so—so *cheap!*"

Shayne laughed and settled comfortably on the sofa close to her. "Don't worry. MacFarlane doesn't want publicity any more than you do."

She moved closer and buried her face convulsively against his shoulder, tugging at his long arm to draw it around her waist.

Shayne had the beer mug to his lips when he felt her squirm against him. He heard the sound of ripping cloth. Then, a wild scream as she stood up and raked her finger nails across his cheek. The torn bodice of her dress came open showing one white breast. Her braids tumbled down, and in the space of a few seconds she was a disheveled and outraged young girl, clinging to him now with surprising strength.

He heard a door opening as he thrust her away. She threw herself at him, pulling his arm around her waist.

There was the flare of a flashlight bulb and Shayne looked up to see two men grinning at him from the doorway leading into the lavatory. One of them was lowering a camera and the other held an ugly short-barreled gun trained on Shayne's belly.

Chapter Eight: A MUG WON'T LISTEN

SHAYNE REACHED FOR HIS POCKET to get a handkerchief and the gunman yelled, "Keep your hands in sight," as he caught the edge of it and flipped it out, then held it against his scratched face. He laughed shortly as the girl cringed away from him, covering her face with one hand while she pulled her dress together in front.

"That was nicely maneuvered, sister. Everybody seems in the mood for pulling old gags tonight. A nice piece of badger baiting." He shot a sardonic look at the gunman. "I presume you're the deacon—this gal's properly indignant father."

"Cut the funny stuff, pal." The man leaned negligently against the door casing, his weasel eyes darting from Shayne to his confederate with the camera. "Go on out the door with your pic, Jake. Get it developed right away. This mug is going to sit quiet until you're in the clear."

Shayne grinned amiably. He asked, "What would the plate cost me?"

"It ain't for sale. Get going, Jake."

Jake sidled toward the outer door with his eyes warily on the detective. Midge was making little whimpering sounds. The gunman dropped his weapon into his coat pocket when Jake was safely out of the room. His thin lips curved into a sneer of triumph. "I guess you know what the score is, shamus. You've pulled enough fast ones yourself to recognize one when you walk into it."

Shayne nodded agreement. He took the handkerchief away from his cheek and frowned at the spots of blood on it. He admonished Midge, "It wasn't necessary to scar me for life. The scene would have been just as convincing without that."

"She did just right," the man in the doorway told him. "That's the little angle that'll really make it tough if you're not smart. A sweet little gal defending her honor against a drunken brute. Boy, was that flashlight one a honey!"

"I'm not in the mood to appreciate artistry right now," Shayne snapped. He pressed the handkerchief against his face again. "You said the plate wasn't for sale. What *do* you want for it?"

"Just for you to get out of Cocopalm, mister. Get out and stay out, see? We've been doing all right here without any nosy dicks from the big city butting in."

"And if I don't get out?"

"That's okay too. You seem to go in for publicity. We'll see how you like this picture on the front page. It'll show you up some different from the one in today's *Voice*."

Midge jerked herself to a strained and stiff position. "Oh—no!" she cried. "You couldn't. They promised me —you *know* Gil wouldn't print that picture."

"Gil's hell bent on printing the news," the man guffawed. "You know that as well as I do. Why shouldn't he print it?"

"Oh, God," moaned the girl. She fell back against the couch, covering her face again, her shoulders quivering.

Shayne laughed unpleasantly and asked, "Why the hell did you think you were pulling this stunt, sister? The only value of a picture like that is the threat of publicity."

"But they told me—they said you—that you wouldn't—"

"That," said Shayne harshly, "is where 'they' miscalculated. I'm not afraid of publicity. But when your dad, the deacon, sees it—"

The gunman snickered and slapped his thigh. "Your dad, the deacon, huh? By God, if you ain't a card, Midge."

She jumped to her feet and went blindly toward the door. Neither of the men made any move to stop her. When she had gone out, Shayne said, "So, MacFarlane is worried about what I'll pick up on the counterfeiting? Tell him for me that he'd better keep right on worrying.

The only way I'll leave Cocopalm is flat on my back."

The gunman's eyes glistened. "Maybe that's an idea."

Shayne nodded. "Maybe so. But he'd better hire a couple of faster rod flashers than those two he planted in the hotel for me tonight."

"That's a funny thing." The man screwed his forehead up in a perplexed frown. "I dunno why Leroy and Taylor went gunning for you. I know for a fact Mac didn't give a damn what you did until you got so set on snooping around out here."

"Why?" Shayne shot at him. "Are the counterfeits being printed here at the club?"

"I don't know nothing about it," the man grunted.

Shayne glanced at his beer mug and saw a small amount of liquid in the bottom. He emptied it with relish, grinning as he set it down empty. He then took up the check for $23.50 and smoothed it out in his big hands. "I've still got to see MacFarlane to tell him where to stick this bill. Where will I find him?"

"I wouldn't go looking for Mac if I was you. Listen, why don't you wise up? If you think that picture's a bluff, you're crazy. Want your wife to see it?"

Shayne's laugh was genuine. "So, that's the angle, eh? Too bad you wasted the plate."

"You're talking through your hat, buddy. You know damn well you can't laugh that picture off." The man moved uneasily, his ugly little eyes filled with alarm.

"Don't call me buddy," Shayne snapped. "Print your picture and be damned." He stood up. "I'm going to take a look over this joint before I leave."

"You better not," the man said desperately. "I'm telling you." He slid his hand into the coat pocket sagging with the weight of his gun.

Shayne laughed. "MacFarlane wouldn't want any shooting in here." He strode toward the door leading into the hall.

The door opened as he reached for the knob.

A tall, ascetic man wearing immaculate dinner clothes confronted him. He had a long face and tired gray eyes which glanced past Shayne at the gunman. He said, "Put that gun back in your pocket, Conway, and get out."

"Sure, boss. Sure. But this mug, he won't listen to sense. I was just telling him—"

"I'll do the telling," Grant MacFarlane said. He waited until Conway went past him and out the door, then entered the room and sank down in the club chair.

Shayne moved back to the couch and sat down on one arm of it, swinging one bony knee over the other. He said, "Don't put too much faith in that picture Jake just snapped, MacFarlane. My reputation will take a lot of beatings without being injured."

"It was an idea," MacFarlane said pleasantly. He opened a leather cigar case and offered one to the detective. He frowned when Shayne shook his head, and selected one for himself. "I don't like the way things are going, Shayne. One of us is going to get hurt if we bump into each other often."

"That's right." Shayne lit a cigarette and waited for Cocopalm's purveyor of vice to continue.

"Why did you insist on coming out here tonight?" MacFarlane made a weary gesture with long, slender fingers. "The Rendezvous can't afford any trouble with the law."

"You forced the issue," Shayne pointed out. "Having your boys jump me in the hotel was an invitation for me to stick my nose in."

Grant MacFarlane nodded. "That was unfortunate." He paused, studying the glowing tip of his cigar. "I presume you wouldn't believe me if I told you they were not acting on my orders."

"Why should I?"

MacFarlane sighed audibly, then nodded. "I see your point. But isn't it conceivable to you that someone else arranged that little scene for the sole purpose of pointing at me if they failed to put you out of the way?"

Shayne studied him with cold eyes. The man's skin was grayish white, his face was long and finely chiseled. His coat sunk in over a concave belly, and his trouser legs bagged over long, skinny legs.

He said, "Keep on talking, MacFarlane."

"You can understand how handy Taylor and Leroy's known association with me would be."

Shayne dragged on his cigarette and let smoke curl from his wide nostrils. "I see the point you are trying to make," he agreed placidly. "But you're going to have a hard time convincing me you didn't send the girl out on the road to bait me into this trap."

"That was after you had already determined to make trouble for me. On the other hand, there's another answer to that. Midge Taylor is Gil Matrix's sweetheart."

"Midge—Taylor?" A muscle in Shayne's cheek quivered.

"That's right. She's Bud Taylor's sister. Knowing you had killed her brother, it wouldn't take much to persuade Midge to harm you in any way she could."

Shayne studied those two fresh angles carefully. After a brief interval he asked, "Are you denying you planned this setup with Jake and Conway—and the girl?"

"Would you believe me if I did deny it?"

Shayne growled, "No."

"Then I shan't bother." MacFarlane spread out his long, classic fingers expressively. "I believe though that I have given you something else to think about—a few questions to ask yourself while you're blundering around in the dark. Leave me alone, Shayne, and you'll be left alone."

"Otherwise?"

"I've always managed to take care of myself." Grant MacFarlane hesitated, then asked plaintively, "Why can't we get together? You're no crusader for purity. I've got a good thing here and I admit you can make a fight expensive—without any gain to yourself."

Shayne said, "I've been hired to stop the counterfeiting at the dog track."

MacFarlane's eyes glowed with a queer light. "Are you willing to settle on that basis?"

"What basis? That the counterfeiting stop?"

"Well, I believe I can promise—"

Shayne said, "No," emphatically. "I don't close my cases that way. Stopping the cashing of counterfeit tickets won't stop me, MacFarlane. It could start up again at another track just as easily. I'm not through in Cocopalm until I put my finger on the counterfeiter."

"And that," MacFarlane murmured, "is what I'm offering to do for you."

Shayne narrowed his eyes and shook his head. He stood up and said, "It wouldn't be any fun to play it your way even if you were on the level—which I don't believe. I'll take my game on the wing—after I've done my own flushing."

"Have it your way," MacFarlane answered lazily. He reached behind him and pressed a button on the wall.

The door opened almost instantly. Conway and another

man stood there.

MacFarlane waved his hand toward Shayne and directed, "Show this man down the back stairs to his car. Follow along and see that he goes directly back to Cocopalm."

Shayne started for the door, hesitated, and turned back to the night club proprietor. He took the check for $23.50 from his pocket and handed it to MacFarlane. "I almost forgot. Take this and hang it in some convenient place."

He went out and the two men followed him down the stairs.

Chapter Nine: MIKE FIGURES THE ANGLES

PHYLLIS WAS SITTING IN A DEEP CHAIR in the ladies' lounge of the lobby, a self-conscious little nook set off from the main lobby by potted palms and ferns, decorated here and there with bright red poinsettia blossoms in tall, earth-filled urns. Her big dark eyes were anxious and a tiny frown showed between her brows.

When Shayne walked in at the front door the frown evaporated as she went swiftly to meet him. She caught his arm, looked up into his face, and the frown appeared again.

"Michael! What on earth is the matter with your face!"

He patted her hand, propelling her firmly toward the empty and secluded lounge. "Not so loud, angel. You see, it was this way—I was driving along the highway, and there in front of me, clearly visible in the headlights, was a little kitten. It looked awfully thin and hungry and run down at the heels, so I stopped and took it in. Now, you know I'm always kind to animals, and I was kind to this one, but believe it or not, it scratched me."

Phyllis's soft young mouth tightened. "Blonde or brunette?" she asked.

"This was one of those little yellow kittens—a common variety," he returned, still patting her hand.

"After this, I'll go with you," she said.

Shayne answered her with a soft chuckle but he did not commit himself.

Phyllis stiffened and pulled her arm away from him as they reached the deserted lounge. "Will Gentry is here," she said in an anxious undertone.

"Now, Phyl, be reasonable," he urged. "Where?" His eyes darted around the main lobby searching for the chief of the Miami detective bureau.

"He's upstairs—in our suite." She sat down in one of the deep chairs and spread her hands in a prim, indignant gesture. "He and Chief Boyle are up there waiting for you. Mr. Gentry sounded quite grim when he telephoned and I said you were out but that I expected you back any minute. I slipped out and left the door open before he got there. I thought maybe you wouldn't want to see him, so I came down to warn you." She glanced up at his face again. "I go to all this trouble when you come back looking like—"

"That was fast thinking, darling," he interrupted. He grinned widely. "Must be something on the Martin killing."

"That's what I was afraid of," she answered faintly.

Looking past her, past the screening palms and ferns and flowers, the redheaded detective stiffened. A deep line formed at the outer corner of each nostril, angled down to his wide mouth.

Phyllis glanced up and saw his face. "What—" she began.

"Oh. Yeh, I heard you, angel." His tone was studiously casual. He turned slowly and looked down at her. "Why don't you run out to the races and amuse yourself?"

"And leave you here—in trouble? No."

"Trouble?" Shayne scoffed. "Not in Cocopalm. I've got the toughs eating out of my hand."

"But what about Mr. Gentry—and Chief Boyle?"

"I'll teach them to eat out of my hand too," Shayne assured her lightly. He swung her up from the chair. "You run along to the track and pick some losers, angel. I'll finish things up here and try to get out for the last race. Watch for me around the jinny pit."

She pouted and then raised gay, shining eyes to his. "I was just fooling about the kitty, Michael. I'll go—if you're sure there's nothing I can do."

"Not a damned thing, angel." He guided her to the door and called to the doorman, "Get the lady a cab to the dog track."

He kissed her lips, then stood in the doorway to watch her disappear into a cab. When it wheeled away, he drew a handkerchief from his pocket and wiped beads of sweat from his face. The lines deepened on his gaunt jaw and his eyes were bleak when he turned back into the lobby.

He walked to the desk and beckoned the clerk with a jerk of his head. "Have you a Mr. Samuelson registered from Miami?"

"Mr. M. Samuelson and party. Yes, sir. They arrived less than half an hour ago."

Shayne said, "Thanks," and turned away. A reckless light glinted in his gray eyes. He strode toward two men sitting close together on a padded bench where they could watch people get on and off the elevators.

He stopped directly in front of them on widespread

feet. One of them pretended to be reading a newspaper while the other was busy cleaning his finger nails with a steel file.

Shayne addressed the newspaper reader coldly. "You boys are off your beat tonight."

The man lifted glacially blue eyes at Shayne over the rim of his paper. He was about thirty with an athletic, well-knit body. He wore a sober brown suit with somber shirt and four-in-hand. His face was without expression, as inhumanly cold as his eyes. He said, "Scram," and dropped his gaze again to the newspaper.

Shayne did not move except to thrust his hands deep into his trouser pockets and teeter forward. The younger man glanced up quickly to meet the detective's eyes. He had sulky lips and his plump cheeks were covered with a soft down. Long, dark lashes added to an effeminate appearance. He wore a wasp-waisted sports coat of expensive material with square padded shoulders. A faint flush crept into his cheeks as Shayne's lips upquirked in harsh amusement. He glanced quickly aside at his older companion and then began carefully inspecting his nails.

In a tone of gentle derision, Shayne said, "I'm surprised Maxie lets you associate with a tough baboon like this one, Melvin. Isn't he afraid Hymie might rub off some of the bloom?"

Melvin squirmed. He glanced at his companion again, entreating him to do something.

Hymie lowered his newspaper. He fixed his glacial eyes on the bottom button of Shayne's coat and advised dispassionately, "Go on back to your knitting, shamus. You're out of your territory too."

"Maybe," said Shayne, "this is some of my knitting."

Hymie shook his head slowly. "Don't push us around.

We got as much right here as you have."

Shayne's smile was bland. "Why, sure. You'll like it here in Cocopalm, Hymie. Only I thought maybe you didn't know I was cleaning up the town. If they start running in gorillas from Miami I'm going to get sore."

Hymie grunted and put his newspaper up in front of his face again. Shayne transferred his attention to the younger man. "When you see Maxie again, tell him I was in Mayme Martin's room this afternoon when she phoned him." He turned and went to the elevator.

The door of his suite was standing open. He walked in and nodded casually to Will Gentry and Chief Boyle. The Miami detective chief was a big thick-shouldered man with a pleasant, beefy face. He and Boyle were both working on fat cigars and the room was foul with smoke.

Shayne asked, "Why haven't you birds taken advantage of my hospitality to order a drink—or hadn't you got round to that yet?"

"We just hadn't got round to it, Mike," Gentry rumbled. "Make mine Scotch and soda."

Shayne turned to the Cocopalm chief, and Boyle nodded with some constraint. "The same for me."

Shayne went into the bedroom and crossed to the night table. He ordered two highballs sent up. When he re-entered the living-room, Gentry said placidly, "That wife of yours puts on a slick disappearing act, Mike. She answered the phone but ducked out before I could get up on the elevator."

"She's determined to be helpful." Shayne grinned widely. "She waylaid me down in the lobby to warn me that a couple of hounds of the law were lying in wait for me up here."

"And you came up anyway?" Gentry squinted at him

through a screen of thick blue smoke. "That means you're ready to come clean, eh?"

"On what?" Shayne went into the bathroom and poured himself a drink of cognac. The boy was at the door with the two whiskies when he returned. Shayne tipped him and signed the check, then passed the tall glasses to his guests. He sat down, swinging one leg over the arm of his chair.

"I think you know what I'm talking about, Mike."

"Maybe I do. Maybe not. Do you want to make a parlor quiz out of it?"

Gentry sighed and shifted his heavy bulk. "A woman named Mayme Martin was murdered in Miami tonight."

Shayne pursed his lips and whistled. "Murdered, eh?"

Gentry nodded emphatically. "The killer messed things up trying to make it look like suicide by using a safety-razor blade. The medical examiner says she was dead before her throat was slit."

Shayne held up his glass and squinted through it. "Why are you telling me about it?"

"Are you going to deny that you knew her?"

"N-o-o," Shayne hedged. "I won't deny that I had met her, Will. But we didn't get very well acquainted. I never saw her before this afternoon."

"She checked into the Red Rose from Cocopalm this afternoon," Gentry told him. "You called on her just before dark—the only visitor she had. Then you came helling up here. What's the connection?"

"When was she killed?" Shayne countered.

"Evidently not long after you went up to talk to her. The doctor hadn't got around to picking an exact time."

"If I had done it," Shayne growled, "I wouldn't have been fool enough to think I could cross you up by slitting her throat after she was dead."

Will Gentry nodded unhappily. "I'm not going to hang the murder on you," he protested. "But she's mixed up in this Cocopalm thing somehow. I thought she might have told you something that would give us a line to work on."

"She didn't tell me anything, Will. She claimed she had information worth a grand to me. That's as far as we got."

"Information about what?"

"This counterfeiting deal."

"I was pretty sure there had to be a connection. That makes three killings in one evening, Mike." He looked at the redheaded detective reproachfully. "Boyle says you hadn't more than reached town before you blasted two of the local yokels."

"In self-defense," Shayne replied cheerfully.

"I know all about that. But the Martin woman wasn't murdered in self-defense." Gentry paused to sip his drink. "Nobody in the apartment house saw anybody else go in or out of her room except you."

"Did you talk to the redhead at the end of the hall?"

"Yep. She says you acted funny. Passed her by when she gave you the come-on."

Shayne grinned, then stated flatly, "Mayme Martin was plenty alive when I left her room."

"Maybe so. But the hell of it is nobody saw her alive afterward."

"No one," Shayne corrected, "that you know anything about."

"Well, yes. You were the only one seen visiting her."

"I know at least one person who saw her after I did."

"Good. I thought maybe you'd have something, Mike. Who was it?"

Shayne shook his head solemnly. "Not yet, Will. I've got to figure the angles."

Will Gentry's manner became brusque. "Don't hold out on me."

"But I've got to see where I stand," Shayne protested. "Maybe I've got something to trade on. If I give it to you I won't have anything left."

"If you don't give it to me you're going to be in pretty deep yourself."

"So that's the way it is?"

Gentry lifted a square, pudgy palm. "I'm giving it to you straight. We found a little something in her room that I think you can explain."

Shayne's eyes narrowed and his face took on a hard, pinched expression. He wasn't deceived by Will Gentry's placidly casual approach. They had been friends a long time, but Gentry never mixed friendship with business. Shayne knew he would get a square deal from the Miami detective chief, but no more than that.

He said, "I'm willing to explain anything I can, but I swear to God, Will, I don't know any more about the woman than you do."

"Are you sure of that? Sure you never saw her before this evening?"

Shayne nodded and growled, "I've never had to prove a statement to you before."

"You've never made the mistake of making one I think I can disprove," Gentry told him.

Shayne's wide mouth tightened. He started to say something, but restrained himself. Gentry was selecting an envelope from among several in his coat pocket. He opened it in his lap and selected a torn slip of paper. He held it toward Shayne and asked, "Ever see that before?"

Shayne looked down at his own name and Miami telephone number written in blue ink on the piece of paper. Below were the two words *Thursday afternoon*.

He wrinkled his forehead and shook his head. "Why should I have seen it before?"

"It was in Miss Martin's purse. It isn't her writing. There wasn't any blue ink in her apartment. It looks more like the sort of thing a man would write and give a woman when he wanted her to call him on a certain day. This is Thursday."

"Sure. And yesterday was Wednesday. Why does that mean I've seen it before?"

"Positive it isn't your writing?" Gentry persisted. "It looks a hell of a lot like the way you write your name, Mike. Boyle and I compared it with your signature downstairs when you registered."

"That's right," Boyle agreed.

Shayne snorted disgust through his nose. "It's no more like my writing than that of a thousand other men. Give it to your handwriting expert and he'll point out a thousand differences."

"I'll do that." Gentry sighed and took the slip of paper from the detective, replaced it in its identifying envelope.

"If that's all you've got—" Shayne began angrily, but Gentry shook his head and held up his hand.

"On top of that," he said, "and maybe it isn't your writing, what happened here in the hotel tonight looks to me like pretty good proof that she *did* tell you something. Are you going to deny that you had advance information that you were going to be jumped by those two torpedoes when you arrived?"

Shayne's gray eyes were frosty with suppressed anger. "Suppose I do deny it?"

"It's going to be pretty hard for me to swallow, Mike. In the first place, why did you take a gun with you when you went to Hardeman's room? I've never known you to carry a gun on a case before. From Hardeman's story, they were all set and waiting for you the moment you stepped in. Yet you came out of it with nothing but a grazed side. Pretty damned lucky if you walked in there without knowing what was coming."

"What are you trying to prove?" Shayne asked.

"That Mayme Martin talked to you this afternoon. She's the only contact you had with the case before you arrived. It must have been her that tipped you off. And if she told you that much, she must have told you a lot more. Don't hold out on us. I know how you are about suppressing information until you're all ready to spring it and clean up —but three people are already dead. Don't be stubborn and hold out until some more die."

"You'll be held accountable if you do," Boyle warned him importantly.

Shayne didn't pay any attention to Boyle. He spoke earnestly to Will Gentry: "Did they tell you that the guy in Hardeman's room who answered the phone told me to knock in a peculiar way so he'd know for sure it was me when I came?"

"No," Gentry admitted, "but—"

"But, hell!" Shayne interrupted impatiently. "Don't you think that was enough to put me on my guard? It sounded phony as the devil—coming from a guy who had insisted on a seven-o'clock appointment on the dot. You know how it is in this work—one little thing will tip off your subconscious."

Gentry studied his earnest face with a hard glance. "Are you trying to talk me off the track, Mike? Didn't Mayme

Martin tell you anything this afternoon?"

"Not one damned thing. Only that she could give me the lowdown on the Cocopalm case, and when I was talking to her I didn't even know there was a Cocopalm case. It wasn't until I got home after seeing Mayme that Phyl told me about Hardeman's call. Naturally I was curious and tried to get it out of her, but she was set on having a thousand berries laid on the line before she talked. You know I'd never lay out a grand without knowing what I was paying for."

"Damn you, Mike," Gentry complained, "you fast-talk me out of every idea I get. I figured I'd have the answer on the Martin murder by finding out why you saw her this afternoon."

"I don't much doubt that the answer is right here in Cocopalm," Shayne encouraged him. "Why not stick around here at least for the night and see what turns up? I may crack this counterfeiting case any minute."

"Have you really got something," Gentry queried dubiously, "or are you just talking through your hat?"

"I've really got something," Shayne insisted with a wolfish grin. "I've just come from the Rendezvous, where I had a very illuminating interview with Grant MacFarlane."

Chief Boyle appeared to shrivel a trifle in his chair. He hastily set down what was left of his drink and got to his feet, mumbling, "Well, I gotta be going. Can't be sitting around here all night while there's work to be done." He wandered out, looking thoroughly unhappy, and Gentry frowned after his hulking figure.

"What happened to him all of a sudden?"

"MacFarlane is Boyle's brother-in-law," Shayne explained. "Among other iniquities, the proprietor of the

Rendezvous is strongly suspected of complicity in the counterfeiting."

"Any other suspects?"

"Plenty—including some of the village's most prominent citizens." Shayne grinned cheerfully and finished his drink. "All I have to do is sort out the right one—and stay alive while I'm doing it."

He got up and stretched, suppressing a yawn. "I've got to look up a local man named Ben Edwards. Ever hear of him?"

Will Gentry stood up, shaking his head thoughtfully and negatively. "Should I have heard of him?"

"Damned if I know, Will. He fits in some place. Want to string along while I find him?"

"I guess not." Gentry laid his hand on the detective's arm. "About your information on the Martin killing— are you sure you don't want to come across?"

"I can't, Will. Not yet."

"Don't frame up anything while I'm waiting for it," Gentry warned him steadily.

Shayne laughed aloud and slapped him on the back. "I'll give it to you as soon as I know where I stand."

They went out together and Shayne locked the door. Gentry went down in the elevator with him, and as they stepped into the lobby, Shayne nudged his stolid companion and whispered loudly, "Don't look now, but do you see what I see?"

Gentry blinked at Hymie and Melvin sitting on the bench where Shayne had left them. Melvin dropped his lashes before Gentry's hard gaze, but Hymie stared back blankly.

Shayne laughed again and took Gentry's arm, led him past the two Miami hoodlums. "Don't jump them," he urged. "I want to see what they're up to. You might get Boyle to put a tail on them, though."

"I'll see if it can be arranged," Gentry promised, and Shayne went out to the street.

Chapter Ten: NO ACCIDENT

THE HOTEL DOORMAN GAVE SHAYNE PRECISE DIRECTIONS for finding Ben Edwards's house. It was an unimpressive frame structure on a wide corner lot two blocks from the ocean.

Shayne shut off his motor and sat slouched behind the wheel for a moment. Two front windows showed light behind drawn shades.

He swung his long body out to the sidewalk and opened a wire gate on a neatly painted picket fence. The lawn was smooth and freshly mown, and there was not much shrubbery, the net effect giving an atmosphere of quiet dignity to the small house.

Stepping onto the wooden porch, he rang the bell and dragged off his hat when the door opened. He faced a motherly woman who studied him with still, gray eyes, then smiled and said, "Yes?"

Shayne asked, "Is Mr. Edwards in?" and she shook her graying head. Folding plump hands over her neat tan house dress, she said, "But I'm expecting him any minute. He's generally through at the office before this." Her manner and voice were patiently cordial, carrying a half-voiced invitation for the stranger to come in and wait.

Shayne promptly accepted by saying, "Do you mind if I wait a few minutes? It's important."

"Of course not." She pushed the screen open and Shayne went past her into a small, well-lighted living-room. A Scottie romped toward him over the clean, worn rug, his tail erect and courteously wagging. He sniffed the cuffs of Shayne's trousers, then allowed the detective to scratch the back of his neck. He retired with dignity after this amenity was concluded. Raising his head, Shayne saw a bright-faced boy of eight or ten who was curled up in a deep chair with schoolbooks and papers. He said, "Hello."

The boy observed the newcomer with questioning eyes and replied, "Good evening," in a disinterested tone.

"You'll have to excuse Tommy's manners," his mother apologized. "He's always too buried under books and papers to stand up."

Tommy then added his own apology, which was a big grin that spread over his freckled face, and resumed his schoolwork.

Shayne turned to the woman and said, "I presume you're Mrs. Edwards." She nodded, and he introduced himself.

"I knew you the instant I saw you at the door, Mr. Shayne. I recognized you from that picture in the afternoon paper."

An animated, "Gee!" came from Tommy. "The detective, huh?"

"Now, Tommy," his mother admonished.

Shayne chuckled. "Do I add up to your idea of a private dick, Tommy?"

"You look plenty tough, all right. Boy! the way you mowed 'em down at the hotel! The Green Hornet couldn't of done no better."

"Couldn't *have* done *any* better, Tommy," his mother corrected patiently. "Won't you take this rocker, Mr. Shayne?"

Shayne said he would. He sat down just back from the circle of light provided by one floor lamp between Tommy's chair and a faded couch. Mrs. Edwards sat on the end of the couch nearest the lamp and picked up a sewing-basket, carefully arranged her glasses which had been laid aside when she answered the door, snipped a thread with her teeth, and said, "I suppose it's something about the counterfeiting you've come to see Ben about, but I don't know what he could tell you."

"Dad hadda go down to take pictures of the gangsters you killed," Tommy put in importantly. "Maybe you've killed some more gangsters since then, huh? Maybe that's why he ain't home yet."

His mother corrected his grammar again and admonished him to get his homework finished. Tommy said, "Isn't," his eyes bright and questioning on Shayne.

Shayne shook his head. "I haven't bumped into any more of them, Tommy." He turned his body in the rocking chair to face Mrs. Edwards. "Is your husband a professional photographer?"

"He takes all the pictures for the *Voice*, along with setting type and a dozen other things." Mrs. Edwards bent her head and began sewing up a split in a boy's shirt. The lamp-glow turned her hair to dark silver, giving the illusion of a bright halo over her head where the new hairs curled up.

Tommy fidgeted in his chair and regarded Shayne with awed eyes, but said nothing more. A smoking-stand by Shayne's elbow held an ash tray. He lit a cigarette and inhaled deeply, let smoke trail lazily from his nostrils. Casually, he asked, "Do you know any reason why a lawyer from Miami—Mr. Samuelson—would be coming up here to see your husband?"

Mrs. Edwards jabbed the point of the needle into her thumb. Her hands jerked and spilled the contents of the sewing-basket on to the couch. Her eyes looked at Shayne steadily, veiled now, and secretive.

"A lawyer? From Miami? Why—no, I certainly don't know, Mr. Shayne."

"Shucks, Ma," Tommy broke in, "that's the name of the guy that—"

She silenced him with a sharp "Tommy!" Her pursed lips rebuked him, then she directed, "Take your things and go to your room. Say good night to Mr. Shayne."

"Aw, gee, Ma, I—"

She said, "Tommy!" again, and he dropped his eyes from hers and nodded. He gathered up his books and papers in silence, then submissively arose and said, "Good night, Mr. Shayne."

Shayne sucked on his cigarette and didn't say anything. Mrs. Edwards gathered her sewing into her lap again and said, "I don't know what gets into Tommy sometimes. He's so anxious not be left out of grown-up talk that he makes things up to get attention."

"Not at all strange for a bright youngster like Tommy." Shayne paused, looking away from the woman, then continued: "But he wasn't making up his story about Mr. Samuelson."

Her toil-roughened hands lay still in her lap. When the detective looked at her he saw abject fright and pleading in her eyes. "Is Ben—is he in any trouble, Mr. Shayne?"

"Not that I know of. Not yet."

"But—what did you mean about the lawyer?"

"I'm trying to get some information," he told her readily. "Max Samuelson is a bloodsucker. He's known as the smartest patent attorney in the South, but I pity the unsuspecting inventor who gets in his clutches. If your husband has an invention, tell him to stay away from Samuelson."

"My husband hasn't any invention." Mrs. Edwards pressed blunt finger tips against her eyes. "I don't know where—people get that idea."

"I got it from Samuelson's interest in him. Maxie wouldn't be putting his nose in the picture if he didn't smell profits."

"Do you mean Mr. Samuelson is here—in Cocopalm?"

Shayne nodded. He leaned back and crossed his legs. "He's in town right now— guarded by a couple of torpedoes from Miami—gunmen, to you. There's something up, and I can't put my finger on it."

Mrs. Edwards moved her head slowly from side to side. Her wide, generous mouth was puckered into a tight slit. "I really don't know what you are talking about, Mr. Shayne. It's true that Ben is—well, he putters in his workshop in the shed outside in his spare time. A month or so ago he got excited when he thought he had made a great discovery—an invention, he called it. Mr. Hardeman suggested that he talk to a lawyer in Miami—about patents and such things." She spread out her hands and relaxed her lips into a tremulous smile. "That's all it ever came to. Ben decided not to get a patent, though Mr. Samuelson urged him to do so. He felt that the lawyer was just encouraging him in order to get a big fee."

Shayne crushed out his cigarette in the ash tray. "Did Mr. Edwards continue to work on his discovery?"

"No. He hasn't been to the workshop for weeks. I do wish he would come home," she added nervously, glancing at the clock on the mantel. "He could tell you much more about it than I can."

"Do you suppose I could get him by phoning the newspaper office?"

Mrs. Edwards arose with alacrity and said, "I'll try. I'm sure he'd come on if he knew you were waiting to see him," and went into an adjoining room.

Shayne heard a car pass the house slowly, stop, then turn in the center of the block and return, gathering speed as it passed the corner.

Mrs. Edwards came back into the living-room looking frankly worried. "Mr. Matrix says he left half an hour ago. He had a telephone call and went out immediately. I don't know where on earth he could have gone."

Shayne sat up alertly. He started to rise, then paused to ask, "Why did you lie to me about Max Samuelson when I first asked? Why did you deny you knew him?"

Mrs. Edwards winced under the blunt accusation. She twined her fingers together in front of her, then faltered, "Well, I—a lot of people here in Cocopalm laugh at Ben about his inventions. They'd laugh still more if they knew he'd called in a famous patent lawyer—and nothing ever came of it."

Shayne nodded, as though he believed her. He got up. "I won't wait any longer, since your husband has been detained. But I wish you'd have him call me at the Tropical Hotel as soon as he gets in."

"Of course, Mr. Shayne. I'm sure Ben will be glad to talk with you."

She went to the door with him, her hand going nervously to her throat while he said "Good night, Mrs. Edwards," and went out.

She was still standing in the doorway when he turned to latch the wire gate behind him, a stout, short figure back-lighted by the rectangle of light, with something pathetic yet essentially courageous in her posture of patient waiting.

Shayne drove swiftly back to the hotel. He strode into the lobby and noted that Melvin and Hymie were no longer seated near the elevators. He went to the desk and described the pair, mentioned where they had been sitting.

The clerk said he had noticed them sitting there. "They were two of Mr. Samuelson's party."

"Did you see them go out?"

"I believe so. Almost immediately after you, sir."

Shayne grunted his disappointment. That meant that Gentry would scarcely have had time to arrange a tail for them. "Is Samuelson in now?" he asked.

"No, sir. He hasn't gone up to his room since registering. He asked for Mr. Hardeman as soon as he arrived—then went out, presumably to see him at the race track when I said that was where Mr. Hardeman could be found."

Shayne nodded and wheeled around. He crossed the lobby in a few long strides and flung himself into his roadster. He paused with his fingers on the ignition switch. The full-bodied scream of a siren sounded from south of town. It expired into a faint moan, then silence.

Shayne turned the switch and pressed the starter. He backed away from the curb, made an illegal U turn and sped southward.

Headlights were converging on a spot in the street a few blocks south of the business district. He pulled past a row of parked cars, nosing beyond the authoritative hand of a distracted policeman who tried to stop him, on to the edge of a circle of onlookers pressed about a crumpled body lying by the side of the road.

An ambulance stood just beyond, and two white-coated men were bending over the body. One of them shook his head and said something to the other. They both straightened up and spoke to Chief Boyle, who stood inside the circle.

Shayne pressed through, glancing down at the dead man. Sightless eyes peered up at him and he recognized the stoop-shouldered man he had seen in the office of the Cocopalm *Voice*.

"I couldn't avoid it," Albert Payson was saying over and over in a flat monotone. "I didn't see him at all. He must have been crouching in the shadow of that clump of oleanders waiting for a car to come by so he could jump out under the wheels. There's no other way to account for it. I tell you I didn't see him. I felt my wheels bump something. My first thought was that I had struck a dog. I came to a stop immediately and rushed back. I was appalled when I saw a man lying there."

"Sure, Mr. Payson," Chief Boyle interrupted sympathetically, putting his hand on the local financier's trembling arm. "Sure, we understand, sir. I don't reckon you're to blame. We all knew Ben Edwards was sort of nutty. Must have slipped an extra cog all of a sudden and chose this way to kill himself."

Shayne turned his back on Boyle and Payson. He stepped back to the body of Ben Edwards lying just beyond a dark patch of shadows cast on the pavement by the moon shining through the oleander. He knelt down beside the body, oblivious of the stares and the murmuring of those who pressed close, made a quick examination of the corpse.

He got up and went back to Boyle, who was still assuring Albert Payson that he mustn't take the accident too much to heart, that it was clearly unavoidable.

Shayne laughed grimly. The chief swung around to gape

at him. Shayne said, "Accident, hell! If you weren't so damned occupied with soothing this bird's fright, you'd know Ben Edwards had been murdered."

"Murdered?" Chief Boyle gulped the word out.

Shayne nodded angrily. "Of course. Don't let anyone touch the body until the coroner gets here."

Chapter Eleven: GOING TO THE DOGS

"YOU GOT NO RIGHT TO HORN IN telling me what to do," Chief Boyle snapped vehemently. "I know not to have a body moved until the coroner inspects it."

"I'm surprised at that," Shayne growled.

Then Shayne felt wiry fingers gripping his arm and heard a panting voice close to his ear, "What's up, Shayne? My God, that's Ben lying there."

Shayne turned to scrutinize Gil Matrix's thin, agitated face. "Ben Edwards worked for you, didn't he?"

"Hell, yes. He was my right-hand man. Been with me ever since I started. Who did this? Some drunken road-hog, I suppose."

"There he is," Shayne said, stepping back and non-chalantly indicating the ashen Mr. Payson. "Boyle thinks he should arrest Edwards for getting in Payson's way," he ended sardonically.

Gil Matrix shouldered past Shayne, tossing his bushy hair dramatically. He shook a long, lean finger in Albert Payson's face. "This is one thing you'll pay for, Payson. You've been running roughshod over people in this town long enough. Strutting around with your potbelly behind the wheel of that limousine. You're a menace to society, and—"

"Shut your mouth, Gil." Chief Boyle pushed him back

with a big blunt hand, blowing out a worried sigh. "Mr. Payson wasn't speeding. You can tell by the tracks he wasn't going more'n twenty miles an hour."

Gil Matrix snorted angrily. "How can you tell? You wouldn't know where to feed yourself if your mouth didn't blather so."

"That don't matter anyhow," the chief asserted stoutly. "Shayne here says it's murder. Says Mr. Payson didn't kill him."

Matrix whirled on the redheaded detective. "Did you make that statement, Shayne?"

"Not exactly. I said that any fool could see he wasn't killed by being struck by a car. The side of his head is crushed where the car didn't touch him. I didn't say Payson didn't kill him. I don't know."

"You just said it again," Boyle averred indignantly. "We all heard you with our own ears. If Ben Edwards was already dead before Mr. Payson's car ran over him, then Mr. Payson can't be held accountable. That's just plain sense."

"It's not that simple," Shayne explained patiently. "How do we know Payson didn't crack his skull first, then lay him out in front of the car and run over him to make it look like an accident?"

Albert Payson's eyes bulged from their sockets. He made smothered sounds of indignant protest.

"You got no right to accuse Mr. Payson of a thing like that," Boyle burst out. "Why would *he* want to kill Ben Edwards?"

Shayne said quietly, "I'm not accusing anyone. I'm pointing out what could have happened. One thing's sure —you're not going to learn the truth by standing here arguing."

"What was he going so slow for if that's not the way it happened?" Matrix yelled vindictively. "He's always breaking the speed limits while you're looking the other way, Boyle. It looks mighty funny to me."

"But this is an outrage." Color was coming into Payson's face and he had stopped shaking. "Completely and utterly fantastic. Why, I scarcely knew Edwards. What motive do you think I could have for such a ghastly crime?"

"You might have been running after his wife. That sort of thing is right up your—"

"Cut it out, Matrix," Shayne said. "That kind of talk isn't going to do any good." He took the little editor by the arm and drew him back, muttering, "Let's get out of here. Edwards's murder can't be solved this way. We've got to run down a motive."

Matrix let himself be drawn away to the outskirts of the crowd, which was growing larger every minute. Shayne led him to his parked roadster, jerked the door open and shoved him in. The editor leaned back and wearily rubbed his eyes as Shayne went around to the other side and got in beside him. He said, "Things are happening too fast even for me. First, those two fellows at the hotel—now, Ben Edwards. Where is it going to stop?"

Shayne said, "Don't forget Mayme Martin."

Matrix turned his head very slowly, as though he feared it might snap off if he made a sudden movement. His eyes bored into Shayne's as he repeated in a tone of choked disbelief, "Mayme Martin?"

Shayne's voice hardened. "Are you sure it's news to you?"

Matrix continued to stare into his face. Beneath the surface of shocked surprise was a faint stirring of relief, as though some realization was slowly seeping through behind the first quick reaction. "Do you mean she—Mayme is dead?"

"Murdered," Shayne amended brutally. "In a way to make it look like suicide. Not so different from the way Ben Edwards just cashed in—indicating a killer with a one-track mind."

"You think she and Ben were both killed by the same person?" Gil Matrix was beginning to tremble. His voice shook with an emotion which Shayne could not quite analyze.

The big detective made a sudden gesture. "Let's get down to cases. It appears that Mayme was killed to prevent her from telling what she knew about the counterfeiting. She offered to crack the case for me, but was murdered before I took her up on it.

"Now, Ben Edwards gets bumped—before I can talk to *him*. You were close to both Mayme and Ben. You were in Miami this afternoon. You knew I was waiting at Ben's house to see him. You weren't far from this spot when Ben got slugged. You printed a headline story this afternoon that set up a slugging for me that didn't come off just right."

Matrix chuckled maliciously. "Trying to hang something on me?"

Shayne hesitated. "I don't know—yet. You're in the middle of it. Too many things revolve around you to laugh them off. Hell, it was even your sweetie who tried to trip me up on my visit to the Rendezvous tonight—after you had sent Edwards scooting out there to contact her."

"Midge Taylor?"

"None other. After her brother and Pug Leroy missed, she took a crack at stopping me."

Matrix mumbled, "I was afraid—" He stopped, jerking his head toward Shayne. "What happened—to Midge, I mean?"

Shayne put his hand up to three long scratches on his cheek. "This is what happened to me—while she was pulling the hoary old decoy stuff for the benefit of Jake's camera."

Matrix's breath grew jerky. He reached for the door-latch. Shayne put his hand over his wrist and jerked it back. "You're going to sit here and talk."

The editor's eyes glinted crazily in the beams of head-lights pointing toward the roadster. He snarled, "You don't know what you're talking about. You don't know any of the inside stuff. I do. By God—"

"That's the reason you're going to talk. I've gone at this thing blind long enough." Shayne held the little man's wrist, forcing him back against the cushion. He growled, "Right now I'm more interested in Ben Edwards's invention than anything else."

Matrix sucked in his breath sharply. He said, "Yeh," in a wondering tone. "I wonder—"

"What about it?" Shayne demanded.

Matrix shrugged his too-big shoulders. "Ask anyone in town and they'll tell you Ben was just a harmless half-wit."

"I'm not asking anyone in town. I'm asking you."

"Ben was a genius," Matrix, apparently satisfied to settle back and talk, said dreamily. "The most brilliant man I've ever met. He could talk fourth dimension while he was completely sober."

"What was his invention?" Shayne pounded at him.

"A camera," Matrix said readily. He paused and a sly expression of triumph came to his face. "This changes things—Ben's death. I've got to see how it fits in."

There was movement all around Shayne's roadster. People surging back and forth excitedly, talking loudly and asking questions which were not answered.

A man leaned across the door on Shayne's left. Shayne turned his head and looked into Hymie's eyes, not six inches from his own. Melvin stood a foot behind his companion. Both the lad's hands were bunched in his coat pockets. His eyes were sultry and venomous.

Hymie said, "The boss wants to see you. Come on." He spoke the words so softly that Matrix did not hear them.

The detective looked past Hymie at Melvin. He laughed. "So you're on the junk again? You're pretty young to go for that stuff."

Melvin's breath hissed out and he said three words which brought Shayne out of the car with his gray eyes blazing and his big fists doubled.

Hymie said, "Shut up, Melvin," and caught Shayne's arm with one hand while the other jammed a gun in his ribs. "Melvin gets like that," he continued mildly. "Let's go, Shayne."

Melvin circled Shayne and came up behind him. His hands were still clenched on the guns in his coat pockets. Hymie led Shayne toward a bright blue sedan parked on the east side of the road south of the death scene. The round end of a cigar glowed from the rear seat.

Shayne waited until Hymie leaned forward to open the door. He took a quick backward step, swinging his right arm high in the air and backward while his left arm circled Hymie's neck.

His right arm settled around Melvin's neck and he swung the two heads together. They made a loud thud, and Melvin wilted to the ground Hymie ducked and backed away, but Shayne's right fist caught the point of his retreating chin. Hymie collapsed against the side of the sedan.

Shayne dropped to his knees as Hymie fell. He unclasped Melvin's fingers from two heavy-caliber guns with barrels sawed off close to the cylinders, stood up and hurled them over the blue sedan into the thick growth of palmettos beyond the roadside.

He then thrust his head inside the rear door of the car and growled to Max Samuelson, "Next time you want to see me, come yourself," slamming the door shut as he finished speaking.

When Shayne stalked up to his roadster, Matrix was sitting where he had left him. The editor greeted his return with a surprised smile. "I hadn't quite made up my mind what I should do. Those fellows appeared quite determined."

Shayne growled an unintelligible reply as he got into the car and started the motor. He pressed the horn down and held it while he jockeyed right and left through the crowd and passed beyond the scene of the accident.

Hymie was sitting up by the blue sedan rubbing his jaw, but Melvin lay still on the ground when they passed.

Shayne smiled grimly and pressed his big foot on the accelerator, and Matrix asked, "Where are we going now?"

Shayne answered morosely, "To the dogs."

Matrix subsided against the cushion and didn't ask any more questions.

Chapter Twelve: A JUMBLE OF SIGNPOSTS

AT THE GREYHOUND TRACK Shayne swung into a floodlighted parking-lot where rows and rows of sleek automobiles were parked in precise ranks. He disregarded the importunate gestures of a uniformed attendant who waved him toward a vacant spot far in the rear of the lot. Instead, he made a circle and parked his roadster near an exit, blocking it so that he couldn't be blocked from getting out through the gate.

The attendant hurried toward him, exclaiming in a shocked tone, "You can't park there, sir. It's against the rules."

Shayne laughed, took the keys from the ignition and went with Gil Matrix toward the revolving entrance. The girl at the ticket window called Matrix by name, smiled, and waved them in without tickets.

A blast of sound welled up from the high-walled enclosure. It was the interval between the third and fourth races, and a ten-piece band was valiantly striving to make itself heard above the voices of the thousands of spectators who had won or lost on the third race.

The orchestra ceased for a brief interval while bugles sounded sharply, then resumed a swing march as tall young men caparisoned like Mexican generals began parading the entrants for the fourth race past the grandstands.

Shayne shouldered his way through the milling crowds about the jinny pit, his eyes darting over the throng, muttering to his companion, "My wife is supposed to be here somewhere."

"Is that why you dragged me out here?" Matrix protested. "I thought you were on the trail of counterfeits."

Shayne gestured impatiently toward the long lines of lucky bettors edging up to the pay-off windows. "A man would have one hell of a time picking a counterfeit ticket out of that mob. No," he went on briskly, "I brought you along to stay out here and watch for my wife while I see Hardeman. After I see him I'll have some more questions for you."

"Go ahead," Matrix agreed willingly. "I'll nab on to your wife if she shows up. H-m-m, let me think, now. She was wearing a white sports dress with a flamingo scarf—unless she changed."

"And a white fur jacket." He nodded and left Matrix standing on tiptoe searching the sea of faces around him.

He shouldered through the lines at the pay-off windows and past lines already beginning to form at the selling-windows. A hectic and jovial informality characterized the night crowd as distinguished from the air of hauteur which pervades the scene at the horse races, for grey-hound racing is truly a sport for the masses.

An arrow said *Offices* and pointed underneath the grandstand. Shayne followed the arrow and opened a door onto a narrow hall with offices on each side. He stuck his head into the first office and asked, "Where is the manager?"

A blond young man stopped rattling a calculating machine long enough to say, "Third door on your left."

Shayne went to the third door on his left and knocked, then turned the knob and walked in. John Hardeman swung about in a swivel chair and looked at Shayne across a littered flat-topped desk. The track manager had been typing with one rubber-covered forefinger at a typewriter stand behind him. He slowly peeled the rubber tip from his finger and said, "Oh, it's you, Mr. Shayne," in a tone of fretful annoyance.

Shayne pulled a straight chair close to the desk. It was comparatively quiet in Hardeman's office, though a dull and unceasing rumble of sound rolled in through an open window behind the desk.

"What progress are you making?" Hardeman leaned back in his swivel chair, putting his palms flat on the desk. "I hope you have something to report."

Shayne shook his head. "I'm not ready to make a report yet." He lit a cigarette and spun the match away. "Did Max Samuelson find you?"

"Yes, he—What's that? Mr. Samuelson? Why, yes. He was in to see me a short time ago. I thought at first I hadn't understood you. I didn't think of you two being acquainted."

"Oh, yes. Maxie and I are old enemies. What did he want?"

"Well, really, Mr. Shayne—" John Hardeman pursed his lips. "I don't see how that can possibly have any connection with your work up here."

"Maybe it hasn't," Shayne growled, "but I'm playing a hunch."

"Of course, I don't mind telling you. It's an open secret that Mr. Samuelson is much interested in the camera invention Ben Edwards has perfected. I happened to be the means of introducing them some weeks ago, and Mr. Samuelson came to confer with me before seeing Edwards again tonight."

"What sort of an invention is it?"

"It's quite complicated. I don't profess to understand the details. An instrument for long-range work with a new type of telescopic lens developed by Edwards over many years of research. I believe there are also many other novel features of automatic precision focusing."

"Does Edwards hold any patents on it?"

"None whatever. That is the utterly incomprehensible situation. Though he has been assured by Attorney Samuelson that it might well be worth millions, he refuses to apply for a patent. None of us can understand his attitude. When I first suggested Samuelson as a patent lawyer, Edwards seemed eager enough to secure patents, but after a couple of conferences he decided, for no reason at all, to drop the entire matter. He now declares the idea unworkable, though that is absurd because he showed me a model in Matrix's office one day—showed me, also, pictures taken automatically of interiors of hotel rooms across the street which brought every tiny detail out with sharp clarity. I was so impressed by those samples of its work that I advised him to get in touch with Mr. Samuelson at once."

"And that was several weeks ago," Shayne mused. "Before the counterfeiting began?"

"Yes. Since then I've been so worried—my time has been so taken up with more important matters that I really haven't had the time or the energy to worry about the affairs of a half-baked inventive genius."

"What did Samuelson want tonight?"

"He wanted my advice on a new plan of attack. Since Edwards refuses to secure patents in his own name, Samuelson is prepared to make him a cash offer for the entire idea. The—ah—working model and plans. He admits it is a highly speculative venture, though it might well prove profitable if the machine is all it has been represented to be."

"What did you advise him?"

"I refused to commit myself. After all, I have no ulterior interest in the device one way or another."

Hardeman rose and glanced at his watch. He frowned and rubbed an exasperated hand over his high forehead, then began pacing up and down the room.

Shayne leaned back and watched him, his brow furrowed with thought. "Tell me if I'm in the way here," he suggested casually.

"Not at all. I have an appointment with Mr. Payson—an appointment already fifteen minutes past due," the track manager ended severely.

Shayne asked, "Does Payson take an active interest in the business affairs of the track?"

"Not normally. I have always handled things to the board's satisfaction until this counterfeiting situation arose." Hardeman sighed deeply, pacing back and forth. "Since then Mr. Payson has been working with me closely. I'm anxious now to learn from him why the ticket design wasn't changed this afternoon. I had to be out of town and trusted him to see to it."

"He was out of town also." Shayne chuckled. "Though I believe he would prefer the fact not made public."

Hardeman said, "Ah," as though he understood. A sudden, full-throated roar came through the open window, the immemorial cry of racing enthusiasts at the start of each race.

"The fourth race—on schedule," Hardeman murmured, glancing at his watch.

Shayne got up from his chair. "I wouldn't wear myself out pacing up and down waiting for Mr. Payson. He's likely to be detained for some time."

"Is that so? Did he send me some message by you?"

"No," Shayne said grimly. "He should be making bond right now if Chief Boyle is on the job."

"Boyle? What—?"

"Payson is involved in—an accident. He calls it an accident. I'm not so sure. At any rate, Ben Edwards is dead and Payson's car ran over his body."

"Ben Edwards—dead?" Hardeman's voice cracked on a

high note. He appeared thoroughly shaken. He stared at Shayne for a long moment, then demanded hoarsely, "Why do you sit around and let people be killed in wholesale lots? Good Lord, man, why don't you do something? Make an arrest—anything to stop this carnival of crime."

"Whom shall I arrest?" Shayne asked him quietly.

Hardeman stopped in front of the desk and rested trembling hands on it. He stared at the detective in disbelief. "Do you mean to say you haven't guessed yet? Are you completely deaf and blind?"

"What the hell do you mean?" Shayne snarled. "I've been on the job a couple of hours, and every time I get the glimmer of an idea it goes to hell the next minute."

"But don't you *know*? Can't you see how everything points to just one man?"

"I can't. Thus far I've met signposts pointing in every direction."

Hardeman's jaw sagged. "But I had hoped— when you said you talked to Mayme Martin in Miami this afternoon—I had an idea you got important information from her."

"Who gave you that idea?"

"I didn't know Miss Martin intimately," Hardeman told him with sudden dignity. "But I chanced to pick her up on the road one night last week when she was more or less intoxicated. She persisted in assuring me that she knew the counterfeiter, knew some fact that would point him out incontrovertibly. She refused, however, to elucidate further, though I confess I received the impression that she knew what she was talking about and might be able to make important revelations if she could be persuaded to talk."

"I agree with you," Shayne answered. "The trouble was,

she wanted a thousand bucks for her information. I didn't know anything about the case, and I refused."

"She demanded a thousand dollars?"

"That's right. Before she'd spill a word." Shayne shrugged. "Somebody shut her mouth for good before I changed my mind."

John Hardeman shook his head sadly. "I'm inclined to believe you were overcautious, Mr. Shayne. I feel sure she possessed some secret information of genuine value."

"All right," Shayne snapped, "maybe I pulled a boner. If so, it wouldn't be the first one. No use crying about it. Mayme's information will be buried with her."

Hardeman appeared deeply shaken by this turn of affairs. He said, "Yes, after I talked with you I heard about Miss Martin's death, though I understood it was suicide. I didn't realize at the time how really unfortunate it was, since you had given me to believe you had discussed the case with her before coming up. At that time I believed you were merely checking her information for correctness and would be ready to take some positive action almost at once."

"How does Edwards's death fit in?" Shayne demanded. "What possible tie-up did he have with the counterfeiting?"

Hardeman heaved a deep sigh as he resumed his seat in the swivel chair. He appeared to have aged years in a few minutes.

"I hardly know," he muttered. "I suppose you know he's on the *Voice* staff. His work and his invention were the poor fellow's only vices."

"He's a printer, of course," Shayne suggested dubiously. "The forgeries are printed—somewhere."

"Quite true. But, Mr. Shayne, it seems to me that the

crux of the affair is the manner in which our counterfeiter learns of the changes to be made in the tickets each day. It is positively incredible how that information leaks out."

Shayne said, "Matrix suspects Boyle of passing on the dope to his brother-in-law, MacFarlane."

Hardeman scowled and said, "Matrix!" in a tone of harsh contempt. "The man simply has a phobia about MacFarlane. He's been crusading editorially against the Rendezvous for a year. He will be particularly bitter now that young Taylor came to such an end tonight, for Matrix is said to be in love with Taylor's sister."

Shayne said, "Yeah. I've met Midge Taylor." He went toward the door. "I've got to find my wife and get her away from here before she loses all of that fee I haven't earned yet."

He nodded to the race-track manager and went out.

Chapter Thirteen: THE TIDE ROLLS IN

APPROACHING THE JINNY PIT, Shayne caught a glimpse of Phyllis's shining, ecstatic face framed by an absurd little white hat that gave her the youthful appearance of a high-school girl at a football game. Her white fur chubby hung open, revealing the scarlet scarf which vied with her cheeks for color. He wondered, fleetingly, whether she had been questioned at the betting windows regarding her age, in keeping with the state law against selling tickets to minors. She was clinging to Gil Matrix's arm, her head level in height with his, though Shayne suspected she stood on tiptoe as she peered anxiously in all directions.

When she saw him towering above the throng, she dragged the editor toward him. She laughed triumphantly up into his face and showed him a sheaf of bills in her purse, cajoling:

"Don't take me away now, Michael. I'm having a wonderful time. I'm winning! Honestly!"

Shayne looked steadily at her, his eyes roving from the top of her little hat to the tips of her white sports shoes. His gaunt face softened and a smile quirked his wide mouth. He said, with excessive gravity, to Matrix, "We'd better turn her over to the police for investigation. The only way she could possibly win would be to get hold of a batch of counterfeit tickets."

"Don't you believe it, Mr. Matrix." Her dark eyes danced merrily. "I met the most fascinating tipster—just a kid, and he looked like a jockey. He gave me a winner in every race, and he gets his dope right from the dogs."

"So-o-o." Shayne grinned. "He reads their mail, eh? Knows what their instructions are." He circled the fur jacket sleeve with one of his big hands and led her toward an exit. "For once in your life you're going to quit a winner."

"But, Michael," she wailed, then stole a look at his face. His features had hardened into set lines again. She made no other protest but went submissively with him.

"You look as though you're on a hot scent," Matrix suggested, stretching out his short legs to keep up with Shayne's long strides.

Shayne grunted, "It's getting warm," and jerked open the door of his roadster. He helped Phyllis in, then went around and got under the wheel. Matrix got in on the other side beside Phyllis.

"I've got to see a lot of people in a hurry," Shayne announced as he surged the roadster forward onto the highway.

"You should have to," Matrix said shortly, "if you haven't picked up any suspect besides me."

"I was coming back to you." Shayne's voice crackled. "I want the lowdown on Edwards's invention. The long-range camera that automatically shoots the interior of hotel rooms across the street. Is it a phony or on the level?"

"You've been listening to Mr. Hardeman," Matrix shot back.

"By God, it was a relief to visit somebody who didn't hedge. I want to know why Edwards refused to patent his invention."

"What difference does it make now? After he's dead?"

"It makes a hell of a lot of difference. He left a wife and kid, didn't he? And it's the key to four killings."

"I don't see how it can be. Just because Ben was a little cracked—shy of publicity—"

Shayne swore fervently, interrupting him. "I've been out to the Edwards house. I met Mrs. Edwards. *She's* not cracked. They don't live too well on the salary you paid Ben. There has to be a potent reason behind Ben's refusal to commercialize his patent."

They were approaching the spot where Ben Edwards's body had lain. The road for blocks around was deserted except for one Ford which stood empty by the side of the road.

Matrix pulled himself up from the cushion and caught the doorlatch. "Let me out here," he said hastily. "That's my car."

Shayne jammed on the brakes and the roadster slithered to a stop. "All right," he said with deadly emphasis, "you know and you're not telling. But the tide's rolling in, Matrix. You can't stop it. The undertow is going to suck somebody under and I don't give a damn who it is."

He waited until Matrix got out and slammed the door with unnecessary force and turned swiftly away toward his car, then Shayne gunned the roadster forward.

Phyllis started to speak but he silenced her. "Watch Matrix's Ford in that rear-view mirror. I'm going to slow up. Tell me as soon as his lights come on and he turns around."

She reached up quickly and turned the tiny mirror lower, watched tensely for a moment, then said, "His lights are on. Now, he's backing around to head in this direction. He—he's coming awfully fast."

Shayne switched off the lights before she finished speaking. Light from the quarter moon sinking low in the west showed a side road shaded with a thick growth of Australian pines. He drove past it, then backed in to the thickest shadow, cut off his motor, and waited, signaling for complete silence to Phyllis.

The Ford whizzed by. Shayne waited a moment, then turned on his lights and drove out onto the highway. The taillight of the Ford showed faintly red a quarter of a mile closer to town.

Shayne put on enough speed to draw up within two blocks of the editor's car and maintained that distance through the business section of Cocopalm.

Matrix swerved to the right on a residential street. Shayne followed, recognizing it as the street on which the Ben Edwards home was located.

The corner cottage was brilliantly lighted and there were three cars parked outside. Matrix sped by without slowing, drove on to a narrow paved road which paralleled the ocean shore, where he swung sharply to the left again.

Shayne slowed between rows of small beach cottages lining both sides of the road, with the surf rolling within a few feet of the foundations of the row to the east. He allowed Matrix to gain two more blocks while a deep frown of perplexity creased his forehead. The cottages became more straggling, and the pounding of surf on the shore was a low continuous rumble.

"Now, where would he be going?" Phyllis asked anxiously.

"I don't know, but it's important, angel."

The Ford slowed, then stopped in front of a beach cottage where a porch light was burning. The light went off when the car stopped.

Shayne cut off his motor and his lights. He relaxed behind the wheel and crushed out his cigarette.

"So what?" Phyllis demanded in a taut voice. "Have you forgotten what to do when you park with me on the beach on a moonlight night?"

Shayne put his right arm around her and she relaxed with a brief sigh. While he continued to watch the cottage and the Ford, he muttered, "I don't understand any of this any more than you do, angel."

She shivered inside the circle of his arm. "Do you think Mr. Matrix is guilty?"

"Your guess is as good as mine right now," he told her. "I'll know more about that when I find out who lives in that cottage. I'll give him a little more time—"

He swore softly when the lights of the editor's Ford blinked on suddenly. Without turning on his own lights he stepped on the starter and pulled forward slowly. When the Ford's taillight whisked around the first corner, back toward Cocopalm, Shayne stepped on the accelerator, then came to an abrupt stop in front of the cottage before which the Ford had been parked.

Phyllis put her hand on Shayne's arm. "There's a

woman in that cottage," she whispered. "I just saw her go past the window."

"I suppose that means I'll have to be chaperoned if I go in," he said lightly. He opened the door and got out. Phyllis sat back against the seat pouting prettily.

"I mean it," he urged. "I may need chaperoning if it's who I think it is."

Phyllis scrambled out and joined him on the shell walk leading up to the front door. "I'm so used to being left behind I didn't suppose you'd want me along. I thought you were kidding me." She gripped his arm with suppressed excitement as they stepped onto the porch. Shayne knocked when he couldn't find an electric button to push.

Swift footsteps sounded inside. The door opened a crack and Shayne pushed it on open against Midge Taylor's slight weight.

She exclaimed, "Oh! It's you," and stepped back, her wide blue eyes burning into his.

Shayne's arm, to which Phyllis held tightly, pulled her forward. "I brought along my wife as a referee if you attack me again." He laughed down into Phyllis's surprised face. "This is Miss Taylor, Mrs. Shayne. Miss Taylor is responsible for these scratches on my cheek. She'll tell you all about it."

Midge stepped backward along the wall, groping with one hand like a drunkard searching for something to hold to. Her honey-colored hair was again coiled smoothly around her head in big braids. She was deathly pale. She had changed from the torn white silk dress to a clean wash frock with white ruffles on the sleeves and it made her look smaller and younger. The simple dress rid her of every hint of sophisticated poise and gave her an ingenuously domestic appearance.

Shayne tossed his hat on a chair and ruffled his red hair irritably. "Stop backing away as though you expect me to pounce on you."

"Don't talk to her like that," Phyllis reprimanded. She went to the girl's side and took her unresisting arm. "Sit down here." She drew Midge down beside her on an old rattan couch which was damp and sticky with salt air, demanding of her husband in an undertone, "Can't you see you frightened her to death barging in like that? She's about to faint."

"No," Midge protested. "I'm—all right. Really I am." She drew her arm away from Phyllis, stared up at Shayne with taut defiance. "I should think you'd be ashamed to come here after what you did tonight. You—oh, you *brute.*" Tears gushed from her eyes and streamed down her pale cheeks. She slumped back, her mouth working convulsively, her hands balled into fists. Slowly she relaxed, gaining control of her tears.

Shayne watched her narrowly, his fingers touching the scratches her nails had left on his cheek. He stood in the center of the small room, and after a time he said harshly, "I suppose you had reference to what happened to your brother?"

"Yes—I— Oh, God! how can you stand there and gloat like that? Bud wasn't bad—not really. I could have—I was trying so hard to make something of him."

Shayne's brows came together in an angry scowl.

Phyllis shook her head at him in an effort to stop his pitiless attitude toward the girl, but he disregarded her.

"How were you trying to help him?" he ground out. "By getting into the same mess yourself? By hanging out at the Rendezvous and tarring yourself with the same stick?"

Midge didn't reply. Her head lolled back and tears again rolled unheeded from wide-open eyes.

"Your brother," Shayne went on mercilessly, "deserved what he got tonight. I killed him—while he was trying to kill me. If that makes me a brute, all right." He dropped into a chair and lit a cigarette.

Phyllis was beginning to understand dimly. She took a handkerchief from her purse and bent over Midge, wiping her cheeks and murmuring, "Please don't. You've got to get hold of yourself. Mike is right. Your brother's death was of his own making. I know just the way it happened."

Midge took the handkerchief from Phyllis and dabbed at her eyes. She swallowed back some more tears and choked out, "I—I know. Bud wouldn't listen to me. He was so headstrong. I was all he had and I—I failed somehow. I didn't know about tonight until—until after—" She nodded toward Shayne and sucked in her lower lip, swallowing hard again.

"Until after you put on your act at the Rendezvous," he supplied. "Who arranged that? Was Gil Matrix in on it?"

"No—oh, no. Of course he wasn't." Midge pushed herself up straight. "You've got to believe me," she implored. "Gil and I had an argument this evening—about Bud. He told me Bud wasn't worth trying to save. But I knew that Bud—for all his wildness—clung to me—loved me. Everything else had failed, so I decided to go out to the Rendezvous and—shame him into quitting that rough crowd. I meant to pretend I would hang around there— and make him quit to get *me* to quit.

"I had every intention of doing something sordid to show Bud how it felt to see his own sister do the things he thought were smart." She paused, her eyes going from

Phyllis to Shayne, pleading with them to believe her.

Shayne's gray eyes were noncommittal through a cloud of smoke. He said, "Well?"

"Well, Mr. MacFarlane called me into his office and told me that Bud had done something terrible. He wouldn't tell me what it was, except that he was in danger and a detective from Miami was after him. He suggested how I could—to trap you—to make you leave Bud alone. He said he thought Bud would be willing to quit and go straight if he got out of this scrape. I believed him—and that's why I did it."

When she finished speaking her chin was tilted at a proud angle. Her shoulders were straight, her whole manner one of defiance, but her hands were clenched so tightly in her lap that the knuckles showed white against the sun-tanned skin.

Shayne nodded. "All right. I'm willing to believe what you say until I can prove something different. But I want to know this: Did Ben Edwards see you when Gil sent him out there just before you stopped me on the road?"

"Why, no. I saw Ben pass—going both ways. I knew Gil was worried about me and wanted me to leave the Rendezvous."

Shayne said, "At last I'm beginning to find out one or two things." He paused, then the question jumped at her:

"What did Gil tell you a few minutes ago—when he stopped here?"

She recovered swiftly from her surprise. "Nothing, except to talk to me about Bud and tell me about Ben Edwards."

Shayne got up abruptly. He rubbed his chin, darted a guilty glance at Phyllis, and asked, "Where's the bathroom?"

"Straight back," Midge told him. "At the end of the hall."

Shayne strode away. When he returned, Phyllis had both Midge's hands in hers and was talking to her in a low, sympathetic voice.

Catching his wife's eye, Shayne suggested, "Suppose you stay here with Miss Taylor for a while. I'm going to be dashing around."

Phyllis nodded happily. "Of course—" she began, but Midge interrupted swiftly:

"No, you mustn't do that. I couldn't let you."

"But I'd love to," Phyllis declared. "I'm sure it would be better than being alone at a time like this."

"No," said Midge flatly. "I want to be alone. I'm sorry, but I couldn't help thinking that—that you're *his* wife."

Phyllis said, "Oh," disappointedly. She glanced at Shayne for guidance, but he had turned his back and walked to the door. "Well," said Phyllis uncertainly, "well, then, I—I guess I won't stay."

Midge didn't say anything. She averted her face from Phyllis's reproachful eyes.

Phyllis caught up with her husband as he started down the steps. "I don't understand," she whispered. "I thought she had forgiven you. She seemed so friendly while we were alone in the room together. She changed all of a sudden when you came back from the bathroom and suggested that I stay with her."

Shayne patted her hand, which rested in the crook of his arm. His low chuckle held no mirth. When they reached the roadster he opened the door, helped her in, saying, "I'll write you a letter of explanation the first spare minute I have."

He stalked around the car and got in. When they pulled

away from the little beach cottage he muttered, "You're entirely too trusting, angel. Too willing to believe what you want to believe. But don't change—keep it up. It's very becoming to your face."

"But, Michael, she did like me. I'm not guessing about that," Phyllis flared.

"Maybe she did. Under happier circumstances you two might be friends. But she was anxious to get rid of us just the same. I looked in the bedroom on my way to the end of the hall. She was just starting to pack her clothes. It looks as though Gil stopped by to tell her to get ready to skip out with him."

Phyllis's dark eyes glowed with curiosity and regret. "Then you think Gil committed the murders—and is trying to get away."

"He won't get away if I can prevent it," Shayne said in a noncommittal tone. He pressed the roadster forward to greater speed, groped for one of Phyllis's hands and squeezed it. "Life plays dirty tricks on people sometimes. If I were God I'd arrange things differently, but I'm not God. I'm just a private dick with a job to do."

She sighed and moved close to his big shoulder. "Just the same, I feel terribly sorry for both of them. I don't believe either of them has ever known peace or happiness."

Chapter Fourteen: TWO FROM THREE LEAVES ONE

SHAYNE MADE A WIDE SWING at the next intersection, and instead of following the direction Matrix had taken he drove back down the beach to the street on which the Edwards house was located.

As he approached from the east he saw that only one

automobile now stood in front of the lighted house. It was a bright blue sedan. Two men lolled back against the cushion of the front seat.

Shayne drove past without slacking speed, swerved into the curb in the middle of the next block, and got out. Phyllis moved her lips to question him as he said:

"Take the car on back to the hotel. Park it in front and leave the key with the clerk." His voice was harsh, and Phyllis saw that all at once his lips were tight.

She slid obediently under the wheel. "Well, you needn't snap my head off," she told him, half seriously. "Why are you getting out here?"

"Sorry, angel." He patted her hand, then jerked his thumb toward the blue sedan. "I'm going back to see Mrs. Edwards. If you see Will Gentry or Chief Boyle around the hotel you might ask one of them to drive by and pick me up presently."

"But I could wait for you, Michael. Honestly, I don't mind waiting at all."

He waggled a long forefinger at her. "Remember, you agreed to take orders when I'm working. Get going."

Disappointment came into her face, but she drove slowly away. He waited to be sure she didn't turn back, then thrust his hands deep in his pockets and strolled back to the palm-shaded sidewalk, whistling. Curiously enough, the tune was his own off-key version of "The Campbells Are Coming."

He saw the flare of a match from the front seat of the sedan as he approached. He groped in his pocket for a cigarette and stuck it between his lips, then stepped to the curb side of the sedan and asked, "Got a match?"

Melvin's young round face twitched. He half turned to Hymie, who sat under the wheel, and his hand dived toward Hymie's left armpit.

Hymie knocked his hand away. "You wanta give him my rod too?" he growled.

Shayne laughed softly. "Why don't you tell him a fairy story to keep him quiet?"

Melvin began to curse the detective in a high-pitched voice while tears of anger and mortification came into his eyes.

"Lay off him," Hymie demanded. "Sweet mother, what's it get you to keep him riled up? We're not bothering you."

Shayne said, "I get a kick out of making him cry." He swung around and opened the gate leading onto the yard walk.

Mrs. Ben Edwards answered the door. Her eyes were red but she was not weeping. Her plump face was stiffly set in tragic lines of acceptance and Shayne divined that she was through with waiting; glad, perhaps, that the time of waiting was ended.

She nodded and said, "Come in, Mr. Shayne," exactly as though he had kept an appointment.

He went into the living-room and said, "Hello," to Mr. Max Samuelson, whose bald head glowed as smooth as a buttered billiard ball. He was seated in the chair which Tommy had occupied earlier in the evening.

The lawyer nodded without speaking. He was a greasily fat little man with a dimpled jaw nestling among many chins. His cheeks had the appearance of never needing a shave and his jowls were as soft and pink as a baby's behind. Ridiculously tiny feet barely reached the floor, though he sat near the edge of the chair, and rings were embedded in the soft flesh of his fingers, which were playing with a heavy gold watch chain suspended across his front. His belly shivered gently, like a protuberant bowl of jelly, each time he breathed. He breathed heavily now, glowering up at Shayne.

Shayne waited until Mrs. Edwards re-entered the room and took her seat on the couch. He said, "I'm sorry about your husband, but I know your friends have said that better than I." He hesitated, glancing at Samuelson, whose eyes steadily watched him with reptilian intentness beneath ugly mottled lids.

"I really stopped by because I saw Max's car outside. I want to spike whatever plans he has for your husband's invention."

"There is no reason for such an attitude, Shayne. If we could speak privately—" Max's breath hissed out and he spoke with a perceptible thickening of his s's.

"We'll do our talking here in front of Mrs. Edwards. What sort of an offer has he made?" Shayne put the question to the widow point blank.

She stirred wearily. "He offered me a hundred dollars to sign a release on all rights to the camera—to turn the model and plans over to him." She spoke softly, her eyes turning anxiously toward a rear door in the living-room.

"Nice going, Maxie," Shayne jeered. "If she refuses your generous offer I suppose you're prepared to give your mugs the go-ahead to steal the plans and model."

"That is no nice thing to say," Samuelson protested. "I take a chance when I offer a dollar of good money. The camera may be no good. There may be other patents. No one can say until the proper investigation is made." He spread out his fat hands and diamonds flashed in the lamplight.

"Please—don't talk loud enough to wake up the boy," Mrs. Edwards pleaded. "He has cried himself to sleep."

"Your pardon," Shayne murmured. He kept his voice

low and scathing when he turned to Samuelson again. "Why did you hurry up here with a couple of bodyguards after hearing what Mayme Martin had to say about the invention?"

A wary look crept into Max Samuelson's hard black eyes. He put up both hands in protest. "I think that is a matter we should not discuss in front of Mrs. Edwards."

"Why not? Don't you want her to hear what Mayme told you?"

The lawyer's multiple chins shook with agitation. He sat forward and the tips of his polished little shoes touched the rug. "Do you want me to say out loud what I found at the Red Rose Apartment when I arrived after you left?"

"Sure. Go ahead and say it."

"The lady was dead." Mr. Samuelson shuddered. "A shocking sight. Blood spilled on the bathroom floor."

Mrs. Edwards uttered a low moan. She slumped sideways limply.

Shayne jumped to his feet and supported her. He said, "That's a lousy choice of words before a lady who's just been told her husband has been killed," in a low, angry voice.

"It was the truth," the lawyer insisted stubbornly. "I have told no one *yet*. And I expect you to tell no one she called me and requested that I come to her apartment just before she died."

Shayne was anxiously fanning the limp woman with his hat. Her face was stricken and flaccid, wrinkled lids were lowered protectingly over her eyes. Her lips began to move and Shayne put his ear close to hear her almost inaudible words. They were a faint sigh, scarcely formed, like words welling up from the subconscious with such agony that the lips were forced to form them.

"Mayme—and Ben—Gil. Gil—is he—next? Oh, God—did Gil—?"

"What is she saying?" Max Samuelson had crossed the worn carpet silently and was bending over the couch anxiously, straining to hear the woman's words.

Shayne growled, "Nothing you'd be interested in. Nothing about the invention." He shouldered the lawyer aside.

Mrs. Edwards's eyelids flickered and faint signs of color began to creep into her cheeks. Shayne straightened up from her and stepped in front of Samuelson, backing him away inexorably.

"You're through here, Maxie. As far as Edwards's invention is concerned, you're through altogether." He backed the fat little lawyer toward the doorway, continuing in the same cold, hard tone:

"That doesn't mean I'm believing your story about Mayme Martin. You wouldn't have wasted much time getting to her after she phoned. I'm not sure she was dead when you got there. The bathroom looked a lot like Hymie's idea of a good way to get rid of her."

"No," Samuelson breathed. His face was the color of putty. "I swear to you—"

"Don't waste your breath. There's also the little matter of Ben Edwards's murder. A widow is easier to deal with, Max. What the hell were you doing out there on the road in your car when he was killed? You had gone to the track half an hour previously. Where were you in the meantime? A phone call took Ben to his appointment with death. Who made that call?"

"How do I know? How should I guess?" Samuelson backed through the door onto the porch before Shayne's steady forward movement.

"You had better think up a good alibi for the time between seeing Hardeman and when I saw your car parked near Edwards's body—headed *toward* town. Don't tell me you were playing the races, because you never gambled a penny in your life."

"Hey," Hymie's guarded voice called from the sedan. "Anything wrong, boss? You want Melvin and me to take that guy?"

"Sure," Shayne called back. He gave Samuelson a shove that sent him teetering to the edge of the porch. "Come on, Hymie."

Mrs. Edwards stood behind them, swaying in the doorway, her arms forming a cross outstretched to support her. "Please—gentlemen. Please don't wake Tommy."

There was movement in the front seat of the sedan. Samuelson called out through chattering teeth, "No, Hymie. Stay where you are." He braced his short legs against a porch upright and summoned a semblance of dignity.

Shayne whirled around and assisted Mrs. Edwards back to the couch, assuring her that there would be no more loud talk, then hurried back to the porch. Moving close to Samuelson, he signaled for him to continue.

"I started back to town as soon as I saw Hardeman," Samuelson said in a low voice. "There was no time between, when I could have been foolishly killing a man. I waited in Hardeman's office for him to come."

"With no witnesses?" Shayne said. "That's a hell of an alibi. It won't sound so good in court." With a gesture of disgust he turned from Samuelson, muttering, "I'll see you later."

He hesitated at the door until Samuelson's quick, short footsteps died away. He heard the motor start and a car door slam, then he went quietly into the living-room.

Mrs. Edwards was sitting at the end of the couch. She watched his approach with wide eyes that were gray pools of misery, of disbelief and dismay conflicting with terrible certitude.

Shayne stopped in front of her, moodily rubbing his jaw. "Maxie is gone," he told her abruptly. "I don't think he will worry you any more. Later I'll put you in touch with a man who will honestly appraise your husband's invention."

She wet her dry lips and said, "Thanks." Her hands mechanically strayed out for the sewing-basket beside her.

Shayne thrust his own hands deep into his pockets, stalked to the chair near the couch, and slouched down into it. "Isn't it time you told me some things, Mrs. Edwards? Your husband is dead now. The truth can no longer hurt him. And Mayme Martin is past caring. There's only—Gil left."

The widow's left eyelid fluttered uncontrollably. Her hands lay quiet and relaxed on the garment in her lap. "Why—do you say that?"

"There's something behind all this," Shayne insisted. "Something I can't put my finger on." He paused, his hard gray eyes glowing speculatively. "Your husband was a very brilliant man. A genius in his line. Why did he bury himself here in this little town—working for the small salary Matrix could afford to pay on the *Voice*?"

"It wasn't so bad," she faltered. "We were happy here in our little home."

"I don't believe Ben Edwards was very happy. A man with his ability would be embittered and frustrated in the position of a small-town newspaper photographer. Yet he stayed here. Why?"

"He and Mr. Matrix were old friends," she defended

her husband feebly. "Gil needed his help when he started in the newspaper business here. Ben was—happy to have a part in the *Voice's* success." Her voice gained strength and conviction as she spoke.

"And Matrix and Mayme Martin were old friends," Shayne mused aloud. "Now—two of the trio are dead. Only Gil is left. Don't you see that you can't hide the truth any longer?"

Mrs. Edwards shook her head stubbornly. She pressed her lips into a tight straight line. "I don't know what you're talking about, Mr. Shayne. Is there anything odd in the fact that three people who had been acquainted before should meet here in Cocopalm—where people from everywhere come?"

He got up and paced the worn rug, darting sharp glances at her. She resumed her sewing on a boy's small shirt. Her fingers scarcely trembled as she plied the needle in small, neat stitches. Her face was again placidly unresponsive.

Shayne stopped in front of a framed and tinted photograph hanging on the wall. The picture was of a lean-jawed young man and a plump young lady with a determined look of pride on her face. Stoop-shouldered Ben Edwards might easily have posed as the young man a decade before, and there was little doubt that the proud woman by his side had turned into the placid-faced mother on the sofa. Worry over something had turned her hair gray prematurely, he decided.

In the lower right-hand corner of the framed photograph was printed: *Herrick-Lane Studio, Urban, Illinois.*

Shayne turned away from the picture and resumed his pacing. Mrs. Edwards continued to sew and said nothing. After a time Shayne broke the silence by asking, "How long have you and Ben been married?"

"Ten years. Ten years lacking only a few days." Mrs. Edwards's voice faltered, but she went on resolutely: "Tuesday would have been our tenth anniversary. We had planned—we were going to Miami to make a day of it. Just the two of us. A regular celebration." She dropped her hands into her lap and gazed past the detective, her eyes wet again, her lips trembling a little.

He said, "I'm sorry—to bring up memories and regrets," but she interrupted him with a fierce gladness:

"You needn't be sorry. Memories are all I have left of Ben. I'll live with memories the rest of my life. Fine memories—nothing can take them away from me. Ben was a good man—a good husband, and a splendid father to our son."

Shayne said, "No. No one can take away your memories." He went to a chair and picked up his hat, twisted it in his big hands. "I don't think Samuelson will come back, Mrs. Edwards. If he does, refuse to deal with him on any basis. And I'd be careful of your husband's model camera and his plans. As long as they are not patented, any crook who got his hands on them could call them his own."

The widow nodded listlessly. "They are perfectly safe for the time being—in the office safe."

Shayne said, "Good night, Mrs. Edwards," abruptly, and went out.

The street was deserted. The quarter moon was not visible above the tropical growth and houses westward. A strong salt-tanged breeze blew in from the east. Shayne took off his hat and let the breeze ruffle his hair as he walked briskly toward town.

When he entered the Tropical Hotel, Will Gentry

jumped up to greet him. "Where the devil have you been?" the Miami detective chief demanded. "Did you know there had been another murder out on the highway toward the dog track?"

Shayne said, "Yeh. I know all about that, Will. Haven't you seen Phyl?"

"No. I just came in a few minutes ago. The clerk said Phyllis was in, but that you hadn't come back."

Shayne nodded, absently running his long fingers through his disheveled hair. "What date is next Tuesday, Will?"

"Next Tuesday? How the hell do I know. Count it up for yourself. This is Thursday. What do you care? With people getting murdered right and left—"

Shayne was not listening. He was counting on his fingers and muttering to himself. He turned abruptly and strode to the hotel switchboard. "Get me police headquarters in Urban, Illinois," he said to the pretty blond operator.

She scribbled on a pad, looked up at him and asked, "Who's calling?"

"Charge it to my account, Michael Shayne, room three-ten."

"You can take the call in the second booth, Mr. Shayne."

Shayne went straight to the booth and closed the door tightly. He stood drumming his fingers on the little wooden shelf as he waited for the connection. Through the glass door he could see Will Gentry standing indecisively where he had left him, staring at the booth with open suspicion and hostility.

It was stifling hot in the narrow enclosure. Shayne whipped out a handkerchief and mopped his face as the telephone rang. He picked up the receiver and a voice said, "Here's your party, sir."

"Hello—Headquarters, Urban," a gruff voice at the other end of the line was saying.

"Go ahead, Mr.—"

"Hello," Shayne's voice roared, when the operator was about to call his name. "Let me speak to the chief."

"This is the chief talking," the midwestern twang assured him.

"This is Will Gentry, chief of detectives from Miami, Florida," Shayne lied briskly. "I'm calling from Cocopalm, Florida, where I'm working on a double murder. I need your co-operation."

"Why, sure, sure. You bet, Gentry." The chief of police in Illinois sounded suitably impressed. "What can I do for you?"

"Rout your county clerk or recorder out of bed and have him look up the marriage records for 1931. I'm interested in a marriage on January 14, 1931. Got that?"

"You bet. Got it written down. I'll call Alonzo Twiggs right away and check up for you in a jiffy."

"Wire me at the Tropical Hotel in Cocopalm, Florida. Give me the names of bride and groom in any marriage on that date—all of them if there was more than one."

" 'Tain't likely there'll be more'n one," the Urban chief said. "It's a red-letter day in Urban when there's more than—"

"That's fine," Shayne cut in heartily. "I'm depending on you, chief, and I'll see that you get full credit when I crack the case."

He hung up and strolled out to the fuming Miami detective chief. "I just used your name and influence on a long-distance call, Will. You should be getting a wire from Urban, Illinois, before very long. If it comes collect, I'll pay the bill."

"Now look here, Mike," Gentry exploded, "what the devil do you—?"

Shayne held up a big hand and backed away. "I don't know—yet. I've got to see Mr. Albert Payson first. After that I hope I'll know what I'm doing."

"I hope to God you do," Gentry said irritably. "I've got a job to do too." He went back and sat down in a deep chair, an expression of morose resignation on his broad, beefy face.

Chapter Fifteen: OUTSIDE OF BANKING HOURS

SHAYNE WENT OVER TO THE DESK and asked the hotel clerk whether Phyllis had left his car keys there. The young man obligingly produced them, and Shayne then inquired about directions for reaching the Albert Payson residence.

"The Paysons live two blocks north of here, on Main Street. You can't miss the house. It's twice the size of any other house on the block."

Shayne said, "Thanks," and long-legged it out to his car. He drove north two blocks and slowed in front of an impressive two-story residence, swung into a concrete driveway. He was halted by a seven-foot iron gate swung onto a concrete and native rock wall. He got out to open the gate and found it padlocked.

Leaving his roadster with the bumper against the gate, he strode to a slightly lower iron gate which opened onto the wall leading to the main entrance. This, too, was padlocked.

Gripping the bars firmly, he vaulted over it and went up the walk. There were lights in the front upstairs windows, but the lower portion of the mansion was dark. He pressed the button and waited.

He heard a window open above his head and Mr. Payson called down fretfully, "Who's there?"

"The law," Shayne called back cheerfully.

"But that's absurd," Payson protested. "Chief Boyle released me on my own recognizance after assuring himself I was in no way culpable."

"This isn't Chief Boyle."

There was a brief pause. Through the open upstairs window Shayne could hear a woman's voice, subdued and tearful. Then Payson demanded, "Are you the detective from Miami?"

"Yes. I want to talk to you about that news story Matrix killed for you this afternoon."

A briefer pause this time, and in a changed tone Payson said, "Very well. Though you'll have to wait a few minutes." His voice no longer came through the window, but Shayne could hear him saying to his wife, "I haven't the slightest idea, Sarah, but I presume it's something about that race-track business."

Shayne lit a cigarette and waited. The few minutes lengthened into five. Then a light came on inside the door and presently a key turned in the lock.

Albert Payson wore an elaborate black silk dressing-gown belted around his rotund figure with pants showing beneath it and a tieless shirt showing between the lapels. He looked worried and distracted. He held up his hand and glanced behind him uneasily, whispering:

"Please, Mr. Shayne, keep your voice down. Mrs. Payson will doubtless be listening at the head of the stairs."

Shayne grinned at the elderly Lothario's discomfiture. He asked, *sotto voce*, "Is there some place we can talk without being overheard?"

Payson cleared his throat gratefully. "Of course—in the

library." He scuttled before the rangy detective down a wide hall to French doors opening into a small room with uncomfortable-looking leather chairs and cases of books. He stood aside for Shayne to pass in, then closed the doors tightly. "After all, Mr. Shayne, one's private affairs—it does seem to me—" He waved both plump hands to express disapproval, then lowered himself into a leather chair.

Shayne remained standing. He arched bushy red brows at the local banker. "That's the trouble with a murder investigation. It doesn't respect the privacy of individuals involved. You have no idea what stenches we unearth before we finally crack a case sometimes."

Mr. Payson sat very still for a moment. He appeared thoroughly subdued and unhappy. "It will be terrible if Sarah learns of my—er—indiscretion, Mr. Shayne."

Shayne said mildly "You middle-aged Don Juans ought to think about that and keep your mind above your waistline. But I'll do what I can—*if* you'll give me the name of the woman you visited in Miami this afternoon."

Mr. Payson's blobby nose quivered. "I see no necessity for that. None whatsoever."

"Look," said Shayne patiently, "you're square in the middle of a counterfeiting mess and a couple of murders. A key witness was murdered in Miami this afternoon. You were in Miami at the time. You begged the man who saw you there not to make that fact public, professing your reason is to keep a moral indiscretion from your wife. Hell, I'm not interested in your morals. I *am* interested in checking your alibi for the time of Mayme Martin's death."

Mr. Payson stared at him in shocked amazement. "Surely you don't suspect me?"

"I suspect everybody," Shayne growled. "The more I can eliminate, the easier my job is. Do I get the woman's name and address?"

The round-bellied little man squirmed and perspired under Shayne's stalking gaze. Finally he recovered his poise and said with dignity, "It can't possibly make any difference." He gave Shayne a name and a hotel room number. Shayne wrote them down in a small notebook and nodded affably.

"All right," he said. "That's attended to. If you've given me a phony I'll know it pretty quick, and it won't help your case any."

Albert Payson stood up.

Shayne sat down in one of the stiff leather chairs. "Our conference has only begun. Sit down, Mr. Payson. Getting the name and address was a sort of gesture—tying up a loose end. What do you know about Gil Matrix?"

"Mr. Matrix? Why—that his credit is above reproach. He meets his payments at the bank promptly."

"What do you know about the man himself?" Shayne quizzed. "His background—his life before he came to Cocopalm and purchased the *Voice?*"

"Very little. He came to the bank with a business proposition. He had an opportunity to snap up the *Voice* at a low figure. He appeared an enterprising sort of man who would give our city the kind of newspaper it needed."

"The bank lent him the money to buy the *Voice?*"

"Yes. We are always delighted to be of service to the community by advancing money to establish—"

"Sure. I know how banks are that way," Shayne cut him off. "But what did he put up for collateral? In being of service to the community you're not likely to overlook a little item like security."

"Naturally not."

"What collateral did Matrix put up to secure the loan?" Shayne tapped the end of a cigarette on the arm of his chair, glancing up at Payson as he reached for a match. The trend of the conversation toward banking matters appeared to ease his physical and mental tension.

"As I recall, the transaction went through on a deed to a printing plant in Illinois. In—ah—" Mr. Payson paused thoughtfully—"Fountain, Illinois, if my memory serves."

Shayne leaned back and closed his eyes, drawing deeply on his cigarette. "I want to get this perfectly straight," he said musingly. "Matrix put up another printing plant in the town of Fountain, Ilinois, as security for a loan to buy out the local newspaper?"

"That is correct, and not at all surprising. A good many people have mortgaged their property in other parts of the country in order to re-establish themselves here on the southern tip of Florida. The deal with Matrix was legitimate in every respect. We took the precaution to investigate the Illinois property, naturally. It was appraised at more than twice the amount of our loan and was under capable management at the time. Our investment was safe in every respect." Mr. Payson hesitated, then added, "In our investigation I recall that the previous owner, from whom Matrix had purchased the Fountain, Illinois, plant, was in prison at the time, though the details of the crime are somewhat hazy to me."

Shayne glanced around the room at the tiers of bookshelves and asked suddenly, "Have you an atlas in your collection?"

Mr. Payson got up and went directly to a section, returning with the leather-bound atlas. Shayne turned to a map of Illinois and with a pencil located the towns of

Urban and Fountain. They were very close together on the small-scale map.

Observing him impatiently, Mr. Payson kept murmuring, "I don't understand. I don't see what possible bearing this can have on either the murders or the counterfeiting."

Shayne straightened up from his inspection of the map. He asked sharply, "Do you recall the name of the man who deeded the Illinois plant to Matrix?"

"No. I can't say offhand."

"I suppose the deed is at the bank?"

"Naturally. In the vault."

Shayne said, "Get a coat and come with me. I've got to see that deed."

"But, Mr. Shayne, at this hour?" Mr. Payson was outraged. "Really, this is going too far."

"Hell, it isn't eleven o'clock," Shayne growled. "Come on, for God's sake, man. There isn't any time to waste."

Mr. Payson became alarmed. "But why is it important to learn the name of an Illinois felon who previously owned a piece of property now held in Mr. Matrix's name?"

Shayne growled, "Cut out your stalling," and seized the chunky man firmly by the arm.

The banker subsided into frightened silence before the implacable look on the detective's face. He let himself be pushed into the hall, where he drew away from Shayne's grasp and went to the foot of the stairs, calling up in a quavering voice:

"Oh—Sarah! I am going out, my dear. On a matter of serious import which will brook no delay."

Sarah called back some reply which sounded very much as if she refused him permission to go out, but Payson hurried toward Shayne, who waited with the front door open. Payson shucked off his robe and put on a coat which he secured from a small closet in the hallway. He buttoned the coat up tightly about his throat, then turned the collar up to hide his lack of a tie.

Shayne chuckled. Mr. Payson's whole appearance was one of a man bent upon the commission of a crime against God and man.

"I dislike being rushed off in this manner," Payson protested, but Shayne offered no comment. He hurried Payson to the front gate, waited impatiently while it was being unlocked, then rushed him to the roadster.

The banker sat huddled beside him while he backed away and turned to head south.

"The bank is on the corner this side of the hotel," Payson told him after they had driven a block. "I'll have to get the attention of the night watchman. This is most irregular, you understand. Strictly against the insurance regulations."

Shayne drove silently. He pulled up in front of the brick corner structure and Payson got out. Plate-glass windows fronting on the street glowed with lights from within. When they peered in the window they saw an old man indolently swishing a mop back and forth on the tiled floor of the bank's foyer.

Mr. Payson tapped on the window with a key and the old man jerked erect, peering out with disbelieving eyes. Payson held up a key and made motions that were supposed to indicate he desired admission, then walked to the heavy doors and turned the key in the lock.

The door opened at once and the aged night watchman stood in the middle of the floor leaning on his mop and watching them with wary, watery eyes.

"It's all right, Jensen," Payson assured him. "Perfectly in order. This man is with me. This isn't a holdup or anything of the sort."

Payson led Shayne behind the partition, explaining nervously, "The cash and negotiable securities are protected by an inner vault with a time lock, of course. We couldn't enter there if we tried. Not possible. Not even I."

"Hell, I don't want to rob your bank." Shayne's grin wasn't pleasant. "But I've got to see that mortgage in a hurry." He stood back and watched the banker manipulate the silvered cylinders of the locking device. He sighed heavily when Payson finally grasped a lever and pressed it and the door came open.

A dome light came on automatically, showing the interior to be higher than a man's head, lined on both sides with filing-drawers from floor to ceiling.

Payson stepped inside and paced along the floor, scanning the typed legend on the front of each door, pinching his plump cheek and mumbling to himself. He stopped and pulled one out on ball-bearing rollers, searched through the tabs on heavy Manila envelopes, then lifted an envelope with a triumphant flourish.

"There you are," he said, "though I still consider this a needless imposition. Totally needless." His confidence and poise were restored to a degree of hauteur here in his own vast vaults.

Shayne said, "You hired me to do a job," and backed out of the stone enclosure with the bulging envelope. He laid it on a desk and untied the cord holding it securely, drew out a sheaf of papers. "You can find it quicker than I can," he advised Payson, shoving the documents in front of him.

Mr. Payson shuffled through them and almost instantly selected the one which Shayne had asked to see, a legal document stating with a great deal of detail and legal verbiage that the title to property therein described had changed hands on October 15, 1936, from the former owner, one Theodore Ross, to Gilbert Matrix, for the sum of one dollar and other valuable considerations.

Shayne's keen gray eyes stopped on the name *Theodore Ross.* He hastily scribbled the name in his notebook while Payson dug out another document which he smoothed out for Shayne's inspection.

"Here" said Payson, "is the mortgage on that plant as executed by Mr. Matrix when the loan was granted. All perfectly in order as you can readily see."

Shayne stood for a moment with his face like granite, switching his cold gaze from one document to the other. His thumb and forefinger tugged at the lobe of his ear, then he asked, "Who passes on a loan such as this, Payson? Do you yourself have the full authority to act for the bank?"

"No, indeed," he answered with quiet dignity. "I wouldn't care to assume such a responsibility even if I were authorized to do so by the board. Any transaction of this nature is discussed and passed on by the entire board of directors sitting in executive session. Here, as you can see, each of them placed his initials on the margin indicating approval." He pointed out initials scrawled in ink on the margin.

Shayne studied the inked initials for a moment. "I suppose each one of them inspects the collateral offered and passes on its value?"

"Certainly. The care exercised in making such loans is the foundation on which the reliability of any banking institution must be based. You should realize—"

"Who makes up your board of directors?" Shayne interrupted.

"Mr. Newson, the realtor, Dr. Fairbanks, Mr. Hardeman, and Dr. Haynes, a dentist, Mr. MacFarlane—"

"I see." Shayne smiled grimly. "Practically a roster of Cocopalm's most civic-minded citizens?"

Mr. Payson drew himself up frigidly. "I had not completed the list. There is also—"

"I heard you the first time," Shayne said roughly and hastily. He began stuffing the papers back into the envelope, but Mr. Payson rescued them from him and retied the envelope in an orderly fashion. Shayne was waiting at the door for him when he emerged from the vault, locked it, and said good night to Jensen, whose eyes were inscrutable above his mop handle.

"I trust you are entirely satisfied," Mr. Payson said as he hurried to keep pace with Shayne's long strides.

Shayne didn't reply until he was under the steering-wheel and had the roadster headed back toward the Payson mansion.

"I'm entirely satisfied," he said. "Far beyond my expectations, Payson." He had the accelerator on the floorboard.

Pulling up at the banker's front gate, he waited for Payson to get out, then said, "Don't worry about anything *if* your lady of light virtue in Miami alibis you." He waved his hand and drove away while the banker scurried into the sanctity of his front yard and locked the gate securely behind him.

A satanic grin spread over Shayne's gaunt face. The grin was brief, resolving into a scowl which set itself upon his features.

Chapter Sixteen: MIKE LOSES A ROUND

HEADING BACK ON MAIN STREET, Shayne's attention was caught by a flicker of light from a rear window of the *Voice* office. He came to an abrupt stop and stared upward, but the beam of light had vanished. All the windows were dark.

He continued to sit immobile behind the wheel with his gaze slanted upward, fixed on that rear window. It had not been imagination. There had been a faint beam of light up there.

It came again. A sliver of light glancing momentarily against the dark windowpane.

He turned off his car lights and slithered to the curb, slid out of the car and walked up the sidewalk to the southeast corner of the two-story building, hesitated only a moment looking upward, then walked silently back along the side of the building. A gaunt shadow in the illusive starlight and reflected lights from the illumined district around him, Shayne circled the rear and the north side to assure himself there was no exit from the upstairs office except the front steps. No rear stairs or fire escape led downward. He stationed himself in the deep shadow of a doorway which was across the street from the Tropical Hotel, and waited.

Only a few cars were parked in front of the hotel at this hour in the evening before the races were over. He could see into the hotel lobby between looped-back silken draperies.

Chief Gentry and Chief Boyle were standing near the doorway. Boyle was talking excitedly, waving his arms. Will Gentry was listening with a dour expression, nodding now and then and rubbing his blunt chin.

Max Samuelson's blue sedan, Shayne noticed, was no-where in sight. He would have given a lot to know where it was—where Max and his two bodyguards were. The model camera and the plans were upstairs in the *Voice* safe. If Maxie was trying to play smart—

Shayne tensed as his quickened perceptions caught the sound of light footsteps stealing down from the news-paper office. He pressed his body back against the closed doors so that his rangy body blended completely with the shadow. He pulled the brim of his hat low over his face and turned his head slowly.

The door at the foot of the stairway squeaked as a hand pressed on it gently from the other side. It came open cautiously, inch by inch, not more than five feet from where Shayne stood, and his fingernails dug into calloused palms while he waited.

He almost jerked into betraying motion when the door came wide open suddenly. He held himself quiet when he saw Gil Matrix step out jauntily onto the sidewalk, letting the door go shut behind him with a little slam.

Matrix stood perfectly still for a moment, then he be-gan whistling as he went down the street without a back-ward glance, his bare head giving the grotesque effect of an inflated balloon floating along above stout round shoulders which bent slightly forward as if he were pull-ing himself up a hill. A briefcase swung from his right hand and the sound of his heels on the sidewalk died away into the night stillness.

Shayne took off his hat and wiped his face all over with a soiled handkerchief, then stepped out of his hideaway and walked boldly across the street. His eyes darted up and down the street, then examined the cars parked in front of the hotel carefully.

It looked as though Maxie Samuelson, his burly get-away driver, and the sniveling Melvin with itching trigger fingers on both hands had got out of town.

Will Gentry met Shayne with a surly growl when he stepped into the hotel lobby. "Where the devil have you been?"

"Out," Shayne returned almost happily.

"Every time you get out of my sight, by God, something bad happens," Chief Boyle proclaimed loudly.

"What has happened this time?" Shayne asked.

"A ruckus down at the Ace-High picture studio. Jake Liverdink was in the dark room doing some developing work when a thug broke in and knocked him out cold. Smashed up some things and got out before Jake could get a look at him."

"He couldn't have seen much out cold," Shayne parried.

"Damn you!" Chief Boyle snarled, but Will Gentry interrupted:

"We have it on good authority that you saw Jake Liverdink earlier in the evening, in a professional way. The way Chief Boyle looks at it—"

Shayne grunted. "If I hadn't been busy doing something else I might have visited Jake *later* in the evening—in a professional way. I happened to be busy breaking and entering the bank, however, so you can't hang Jake's troubles around my neck."

Boyle's eyes started to pop out. "Breaking in the bank? Well, by God—"

"Aided by the president of the institution," Shayne cut him off. He turned to Gentry and asked:

"Any telegram from Illinois, Will?"

"Not yet." Gentry chewed fiercely on the frayed butt of a cigar. He jerked it out of his mouth and sniffed it, then hurled it out the door. "I can't stand around here all night," he shot at Shayne. "I'm still working on the Martin murder and you haven't given me a goddamn thing. You're still the last man who saw her alive as far as I know."

Shayne nodded absently. "I still think you'll clear it up by staying here in Cocopalm faster than it can be done in Miami. If Maxie was telling me the truth—"

"Maxie? Samuelson? How does he fit in?" Gentry demanded irritably.

"I'll tell you, Will. That's what I held out on you up in my room," Shayne said with unmistakable seriousness. "I didn't know how much pressure I'd need to use on Maxie and I wanted to keep that for myself if I needed it. But Maxie seems to have faded out of the picture up here. This is straight. Max Samuelson was on his way up to see the Martin woman when I walked out of her apartment."

Gentry's beefy face grew slowly livid. "Then Samuelson saw her after you did. And he was here where I could get my hands on him and you didn't tip me off."

"I couldn't, Will," Shayne insisted. "Not then. What good would it have done you anyway?"

"What good?" Gentry was apoplectic with rage. "Hell, I would've put the screws on him. He would've talked plenty to me, he would."

"You can pick him up in Miami any time you want him," Shayne reminded his old friend mildly. "I don't think you'll get much except to set the time of her death closely. He swears and be damned that she was dead when he got there."

"Oh, he does, does he? And you believed him?" Gentry's heavy upper lip curled.

"I haven't got any beliefs yet, Will. All I've got is a theory."

"The hell you have." Gentry's sarcastic tone did not change. "Maybe you'd like to let us in on this theory. We are sort of interested too, you know. Maybe you don't realize it, but we've both had a murder occur in our territory tonight. Of course, murders aren't important to you while you're chasing a fee, but they happen to be our job. Mike, if you don't come clean—"

"I can't. Not yet. Not until that wire comes through from Illinois. Let me know as soon as you get it, Will." He stood thoughtfully tugging at the lobe of his ear, then muttered, "I'll be in my room," and hurried toward the elevator.

The door of the hotel suite was locked. Shayne knocked loudly. After a time he heard movement in the room, then the knob turned and the door opened a cautious inch.

Shayne shoved the door wide open.

Phyllis backed away from him. Her eyes were enormous and stared at him with hot rebellion. She wore a hostess gown of blue silk taffeta which swept to the floor in swinging fullness, rustling at her slightest movement. She folded her hands and stood straight and slim and outraged before him.

Shayne grinned. "Are you practicing up for something, angel?" His gray eyes were laughing. He took a step toward her, pushing the door shut with a hand behind him.

Phyllis put out a restraining hand. "Don't touch me," she ordered shortly. "Don't even so much as lay a finger on me."

The smile went away from Shayne's eyes, from his deeply lined face. Slowly, as though he willed it to remain but could not make his facial muscles obey.

He said, "What the hell, Phyl?" looking down at himself appraisingly, sniffing to assure himself he hadn't inadvertently become smeared with a stench.

"Don't try to be smug about it," she flung at him. "I'll never let you touch me again. Never—as long as I live."

"Hell's bells," he remonstrated, "I'm not being smug. I'm only being confounded. I never felt less smug in my life. What's the matter with you?"

Phyllis sniffled and there was a catch in her throat when she said, "I just happen to have some pride left. That's all. I suppose you thought you had crushed it when you married me."

Shayne put his hands on his hips and studied her with narrowed eyes. She mimicked him by planting her hands on her hips and narrowing her eyes right back.

He laughed, but it was a feeble attempt at humor. "Are you sore because I couldn't get back sooner? I've been busy as the devil, and—"

"I certainly am not," she stormed at him. "If you had never come back it would have suited me better."

Shayne sighed. "If you'd only be reasonable, angel."

"Don't call me angel," she snapped. She stamped her small blue satin slipper on the rug. "Reasonable? Acquiescent is the word you want."

Shayne said, "Hell!" in a bitter, wondering tone. He turned away from her and went into the bathroom, where he uncorked his cognac bottle and splashed a water glass half full of the high-proof liquid.

"That's right," Phyllis called in a high-pitched, hysterical voice, "soak yourself with brandy."

Shayne had the glass halfway to his lips. He held it there, scowling at the clear amber liquid. Then he tipped it up and took two big swallows.

He set the glass down and examined himself carefully in the mirror. His hair was every which way and the scratches on his left cheek did not enhance his doubtful good looks. His eyes stared back at him with a weary expression. The stiff bristle on his face had grown unbelievably since morning.

For the thousandth time he wondered how he had been lucky enough to marry a young, beautiful girl like Phyllis; wondered, with a fierce tingle of actual fright, how long she would be satisfied to remain married to him.

Maybe this was the beginning of the end. A situation like this was something he didn't know how to handle. He had had experience with hysterical women of an entirely different type. But, hell, a man couldn't slap his wife around.

He cocked his ear toward the partially open bathroom door. He could hear her wild sobbing, hear the choking in her throat.

He closed the door silently, stalked back to the lavatory, and took another long drink, looking away from the unpleasant ugliness of his reflection.

He poured more liquor into his glass and drank it. Then he looked around him, saw a cake of Phyllis's complexion soap. He hurriedly took off his tie and turned his shirt back at the throat, rolled up his sleeves, and doused himself with soapsuds and hot water. He found his razor, spread shave cream over his face, and shaved hurriedly, carefully edging the ugly scratches. He doused his bristly hair with hot water and combed it down sleek.

Replacing his tie, he took a last look at his reflection in the mirror and strode into the living-room.

Phyllis was sitting in a deep chair rocking back and

forth with her hands covering her face. Her shoulders were shaking uncontrollably and the sounds of suffering from behind her fingers were unendurable.

Shayne dropped on his knees before her and put a long arm around her. "Don't, Phyl. For God's sake, I can't stand this." He tugged gently at one of her hands to get it away from her face.

Suddenly she lifted her head. There were no tears in her eyes. Convulsed with mirth, her eyes were wickedly bright, her young face radiant.

"Michael Shayne," she choked out, "how you ever got to be the world's best detective I don't know."

His arm tightened around her. Abruptly he swung her up from the chair and sat down in it, laying her neatly across his knobby knees. He cupped his palm to make a resounding noise as it came down.

"I should have done this long ago," he said grimly and in a tone which rang with sheer relief. "Say 'nuff' when you're ready."

"Nuff," she cried through her hysterical laughter.

He swung her upright and caught her close in his arms. "Now, tell me, what's the occasion for all this burlesque? You scared me out of my wits."

"Oh, Mike," she caroled, "you looked so—so woebegone —so *damn* funny when I started in. I didn't mean to keep it up, honest."

He muttered, "Yeh, I guess it was funny."

Phyllis drew back from him and looked at his hair. She ran soft fingers over his cheek, then she ran both hands through his hair and left it standing on end.

"I'm sorry, Michael. It was a lousy trick. But I—I got started and couldn't stop. It was—the first time I realized I could handle you." She gazed at him with round, dark, wondering eyes.

Shayne let his legs down and dumped her on the floor. "Next time you pull a stunt like that I'll whale hell out of you."

Phyllis turned her bright smile into a pout. "Well, I really had cause to put on a scene. You certainly looked as if you were playing for keeps in that picture."

Shayne looked down at her sitting with her knees doubled up and her arms clasping them. "What picture, angel?"

"Why, the one of you and that Taylor girl." She swung to her feet and ran across the room to a small table. She picked up a photographer's envelope and came back, opening the flap and drawing out a glossy print.

"There," she said, handing it to him and dropping again to the floor in front of him. "If that isn't the most shameless thing I ever saw."

The photograph was, as Conway had gloatingly predicted, a honey. Three lines of blood showed on Shayne's cheek and the camera had caught a perfect expression of guilt as he jerked his head toward the flash of the bulb. His arm was tightly around Midge's waist as though he hung on doggedly while she sought to wrestle away, and the fingers of his other hand were curved suggestively close to the torn bosom of her dress as they might have been had he ripped the fabric.

Midge Taylor was drawn back from him tautly, a look of real terror and of maidenly anger on her face.

Shayne studied the print from several angles, nodding gravely. "Playboy Shayne at his best," he commented. "That's an example of the technique I had just perfected when you slipped up on my blind side and married me."

Phyllis laughed scornfully. "That's your innate modesty. You know you never had to tear the clothes off women."

"How did *you* get hold of this?" He reached for the envelope and read the printed legend: *Ace-High Studio, Jake Liverdink, Prop.*

"Oh, I forgot you didn't know," Phyllis said. She sprang from the floor and sat on the arm of his chair, cuddling against him. "Mr. Matrix sent it up while you were out—along with this note." She unzipped the front of her gown to get out a folded note.

Shayne took it and read:

Here's the only print there'll ever be. Keep it for a souvenir from Midge and me. This puts you in the clear to go after MacFarlane and his racket any way you want to.

GIL MATRIX.

A queer light came into Shayne's eyes and he sat for a moment staring into space.

Phyllis looked impatient. "What does it mean?" she demanded eagerly. "Is this what you wouldn't tell me about your trip out to the Rendezvous—when you insisted on talking about kittens in the road?"

Shayne grinned and nodded. "That's exactly it, angel. Gil spoiled the game by breaking into the studio and smashing the plate—as much for Midge as for us, I imagine."

The telephone rang in the bedroom before Phyllis could question him further.

Shayne sprang to his feet as though propelled by a coiled spring and rushed to answer it.

Will Gentry said, "I've just received a wire signed by the chief of police of Urban, Illinois."

"Read it to me."

He said, "Claude Bates and Lucretia Grant only couple married on that date. Now, what the hell, Mike?"

Shayne said, "Thanks, Will," and hung up quickly. He took a notebook from his pocket and scribbled down the two names, then sat on the edge of the bed rubbing his lean jaw.

He then lifted the phone and asked the hotel switchboard operator to get him the warden of the state penitentiary at Joliet, Illinois.

Chapter Seventeen: NO REST FOR THE CORONER

MICHAEL SHAYNE HELD THE TELEPHONE to his ear with one hand and fished a cigarette from a pack in his pocket while he waited. Phyllis came in and sat beside him, struck a match and lit his cigarette with silent competence.

He listened to long-distance operators talking back and forth, and finally a voice informed him, "We are ready with the state penitentiary at Joliet, Mr. Shayne, but the warden is not in. Will you talk to someone else?"

"Anyone in authority," Shayne answered, and after another brief wait the voice said, "Here's your party. Go ahead, please."

Shayne said, "Hello, Joliet," and a male voice answered, "Hello."

"This is Michael Shayne speaking—a private detective in Miami, Florida. I'm working on a murder and counterfeiting case and I think you have information that will crack it for me."

"What information do you need?"

"The dope on a couple of former inmates. Their names are Claude Bates and Theodore Ross. Got that?"

"Just a minute while I write them down. All right."

"I don't know the date you received these men. About ten years ago—or less than that. I don't know what the charge or sentence was, though I have a hunch they went up for some sort of counterfeiting racket—printed forgeries of some sort, I imagine."

"It'll take some time to check the records on that meager information," the voice from the penitentiary warned him. "Do you want it tonight or—"

"I want it right now. I'll hold the line while you check."

He heard a resigned, "Very well," and relaxed to wait. He sucked on the cigarette, staring straight in front of him with brows knitted. Though he had spoken over the telephone with crisp certainty, he wasn't at all certain that his hunch was right. In one sense it had to be that way, but in a dozen other logical answers there might be one that would fit the facts in his possession as well.

After waiting and listening for ten minutes, he said to Phyllis, "It's taking them a hell of a long time to get the information. They should have all the names of former prisoners filed alphabetically. It shouldn't take so long—"

His fingers tightened on the telephone when a voice came through. He frowned and said resignedly, "Yes— waiting."

Then, the deep furrows smoothed out as he listened to the prison deputy. He said, "That's swell. Nineteen-thirty-one, eh? Twenty to fifty years. Escaped in 'thirty-six." He kept nodding while he listened, a pleasurable gleam in his gray eyes.

"That's fine," he said presently. "I've got all that, and thanks. I'm quite sure I'll have something on that for you tomorrow."

With the instrument held to his ear he broke the connection, and when the switchboard answered he said, "I want to speak to Timothy Rourke." He gave a Miami residence telephone number and waited.

Phyllis asked, "Are you going to have a scoop for Tim?" excitedly.

Shayne grinned and gestured for silence. In a moment he said, "Hello—Tim? Shayne speaking. Come on up to Cocopalm right away. I'm about to play an ace that'll win the pot if somebody doesn't play the joker."

"What's up, Mike? Something on the Mayme Martin murder?"

"Maybe. And there are a couple of other angles. I thought maybe you'd want to be in on it since you dealt the hand when you delivered that message from Phyl this afternoon."

"Maybe! Mike, why didn't you call me—"

"See you at headquarters in Cocopalm."

When he cradled the receiver Phyllis was tugging at his arm. "What is it, Michael? You look like a cat that's swallowed three canaries. Who are these men—Bates and Ross? I've never even heard their names in connection with the case."

Shayne stood up slowly and the expression of exultation slowly went from his face. He stared down at his hands, cracking one knuckle after the other.

"It's the roundup, Phyl. I know who's been doing the counterfeiting—who murdered Mayme Martin and Ben Edwards—and *why* they were murdered."

"You don't look very happy about it. Have you forgotten the fee you'll have coming? And who—?"

He silenced her with a long, searching look. "This isn't going to be any fun, Phyl. Someone else is going to get hurt. That's the hell of crime."

He shrugged his shoulders, bent and kissed her lips lightly. "Don't worry. And Phyl—"

"Yes?"

"I wish you'd get dressed to go out. I don't know, but I think I may call on you for a little help after a while."

"Of course." She sprang to her feet, seized his arm. "Is it that girl—out on the beach?"

He said, "Yeh. Midge. It's funny how life slaps some people around."

He went out and grabbed his hat and went down in the elevator. Will Gentry was waiting for him in the lobby. He growled, "Well, you got the wire you wanted. It's taken you a hell of a long time to get down here. Now what?"

"The rest of it is easy. Only—you and Chief Boyle will have to fight over jurisdiction. *Your* man also killed Ben Edwards."

"Who? What the hell do you know?"

"I'll handle the finish my own way," Shayne advised him dryly. "I don't want either you or Boyle horning in at the last minute and spoiling my claim on the fee from the race-track officials."

He stalked away from Gentry and went to the desk. "How long ago was Matrix here—when he brought that envelope you sent up to my wife?"

The clerk pursed his lips and glanced up at the clock. "Something like half an hour ago, I imagine. He said you were in his office waiting for him then."

"Matrix said I was waiting for him in his office?"

"Why, yes. He offered to take the message over to you, and since he was going anyway—"

Shayne's fingers closed down on the clerk's forearm and drew a little yelp of pain from him. "What message are you talking about?"

"Why, the one that came for you by messenger. A plain sealed envelope marked *Urgent*. It came while Mr. Matrix was standing here at the desk, and I thought—of course—"

"You didn't think," Shayne snapped. His nostrils flared and he breathed through them heavily. He dropped the man's limp forearm with a flat, tired oath, then strode to the switchboard and ordered the girl to connect him with John Hardeman at the race track at once.

He leaned against the railing and lit a cigarette while the operator's fingers nimbly put plugs in holes and pulled plugs out of holes. She looked up after a time and said brightly, "I'm sorry. Mr. Hardeman does not answer."

Shayne dragged himself erect. He saw Gentry watching him quizzically but the burly chief made no move to interfere. Shayne went back to the desk and asked the hotel clerk, "Where does Matrix live?"

"One block down." The clerk gestured southward. "The Magnolia Apartments."

Shayne surged out of the lobby and across the street to where he had left his roadster parked when he reconnoitered the printing plant and its strange flashes of light. He slammed it down the street in second gear, screeched up in front of the Magnolia Apartments and leaped out.

Four long strides took him into a small foyer with mail slots all around. Matrix's name was on No. 4.

He found No. 4 at the end of the hall. It was dark and his knock went unanswered. He tried three keys in the lock before finding one that would open it.

He snapped on a ceiling light. The apartment was in a state of complete disorder, with three closed traveling-bags and a briefcase standing in the center of the floor.

Turning off the light and closing the door as he went

out, Shayne walked slowly back to his car. Under the wheel, he paused to light a cigarette and draw on it thoughtfully before putting the car in gear. Then he wheeled around and drove to the hotel at slow speed.

Will Gentry looked up with interest when Shayne approached from the doorway. He started to ask a question, but did not after he got a good look at Shayne's face.

The redheaded detective gripped Gentry's arm and led him to the door. "Will you do something for me, Will? Without asking questions?"

Gentry said, "Sure," and waited.

Shayne gave him the address of a cottage on the beach. "Drive out there and park within a block or so. Gil Matrix will be there after a while. Leave him alone—until he tries to leave the cottage with a girl. If he does that before I get out there, stop him—and wait there for me."

Gentry agreed without asking any questions. He got in his car and drove in the opposite direction while Shayne raced his roadster toward the race track.

A few automobiles were leaving the track parking-lot when Shayne approached, the early-departing vanguard of the rush that would follow the final race, those who liked to avoid the final rush or who had lost all their money through the pari-mutuels and were willing to call it a night.

Shayne drove into the lot, but this time did not affront the attendant by parking for a quick getaway. He slid his roadster into the spot indicated, got out and strode at a swinging pace to the entrance gate, which was open and deserted at an hour when the night's racing was almost over.

The grandstand appeared as crowded with gay costumes as it had been earlier in the evening, and throngs still surged about the betting-windows as the dogs were paraded for the last race.

Shayne shouldered his way among them, grim-faced and calm, went to the door under the grandstand leading to the offices. The same clattering of calculating machines and typewriters smote his ears as before.

This time he went direct to the door of John Hardeman's office. He knocked tentatively, with the air of a man who did not expect his knock to be answered.

It was not answered.

The knob refused to turn when he put pressure on it.

He shielded his action with his body while drawing a ring crowded with keys from his pocket. He tried half a dozen without success, but persevered until the right key came to his hand.

It turned grudgingly in the lock. He glanced around the empty corridor before pushing the door open and sliding into the dark office.

He took time to get the key out of the lock and close the door on the night latch before feeling for a light switch. His nostrils twitched with the lingering acrid odor of gun smoke in them as he found the switch and pressed it. He turned slowly and stared with somber eyes at the dead body of John Hardeman slumped sideways in his swivel chair with a small powder-marked hole in his right temple.

Band music came through the open window mingled with the hopeful shouts of the racing throng.

Chapter Eighteen: WHILE THE CROWD ROARS

SHAYNE STOOD BACKED AGAINST THE DOOR without moving for a full minute. Then he glanced at the open window nd went to it, circling the flat desk and the corpse.

The rear of the office abutted almost against the blank-
ness of a high board wall enclosing the track with barely
oom for a body to squeeze between wall and window.
hayne stepped back, satisfied that no one could look into
he office through the aperture.

He stopped a foot from Hardeman's body, right thumb
and forefinger seizing the lobe of his left ear and kneading
t absently while his gray eyes studied every minute detail
of the death scene before him.

Hardeman's chair was swiveled to the left, halfway between the flat-topped desk and typewriter stand behind
him. His head rested laxly on his left shoulder slumped
low in the chair and his left arm hung down over the chair
arm with the tips of his fingers almost touching the office
floor.

His right hand rested inside the open top drawer of the
desk, barely touching the butt of a Police Positive .38 lying
on top of a batch of papers. The forefinger of his right
hand still wore the protective rubber covering with which
he had been picking out letters on the typewriter when
Shayne had entered the office earlier.

A sheet of paper was rolled in the typewriter behind
him. It carried the printed letterhead of the race track,
with John Hardeman's name in modest letters in the left-
hand corner under the legend *Manager*.

The date had been typed beneath the letterhead. That
was as far as Hardeman had got with whatever communi-
cation he had been on the point of typing.

The single bullet which had killed the manager had
not come out the back of his head. There was only the
wound, pockmarked with powder burns all around, a
little above and halfway between his right ear and eye.

Blood had run from the wound and made a path down Hardeman's cheek to the point of his chin, where it dripped off to the rug.

Blood continued to dribble from the wound as Shayne stood there. Single thick drops, widely spaced as the fluid clotted. It fell with a dull plopping sound into the thickening pool directly beneath.

It was a simple matter to reconstruct the exact manner in which John Hardeman had met his death. He had been turned away from his desk typing with the rubber-covered forefinger when someone entered his office. The door had been unlocked, Shayne recalled, on his previous visit.

Swiveling about to face his visitor, the race-track manager had looked into the muzzle of a gun. His instinctive reaction had been to make a desperate reach for his own pistol, which lay conveniently at hand in the open drawer. He had died before his fingers could grasp the weapon.

Everything else in the office was the same as Shayne had seen it before. Apparently nothing had been tampered with in any way. Hardeman's killer must have fled furtively as soon as the lethal shot was fired. It was entirely practicable to enter and leave the private office via the hallway unnoticed, as Shayne was fully aware.

After a thorough inspection of the dead man, Shayne stopped rolling his earlobe and stepped back. He hooked one thigh over a corner of Hardeman's desk and considered the situation carefully, in respect to himself, and as it had a bearing on two other murders and the conclusion he had worked out in his mind for the case.

A queer hot light flickered in his gray eyes. They stared unblinkingly at the dead figure before him. A grim look of questioning came over his face. He got up and approached Hardeman again, turned back his coat, and nodded at sight of a leather wallet in the dead man's inside breast pocket.

He hesitated, then whisked out a handkerchief and draped it over his fingers, gingerly drew the wallet out and went back to sit on the desk.

Using his handkerchief to prevent his own fingerprints being left behind, he opened the wallet and emptied the inner compartments of a miscellany of cards, receipts, and folded memoranda onto the desk.

Among them was a folded clipping from a newspaper. It was somewhat faded and brittle with age, beginning to crack in the folds. He smoothed it out carefully and his eyes brooded over a blurred halftone and the brief news story beneath.

With the handkerchief still guarding his fingers, he awkwardly gathered the other papers and cards and returned them to Hardeman's wallet, replaced it in his coat pocket.

Shayne's step had an elastic, springy quality as he turned back to the desk, as though he stalked a prey now certainly within his power.

The newspaper cut showed a picture of two men standing side by side. On the left was a lean-jawed man similar to the tinted wedding photograph hanging on the wall of Ben Edwards's home. The man on the right had a dwarfish body with thin intense features and a big head made to appear bigger by bushy uncombed hair. The features were those of Gil Matrix a decade before.

The cut-line beneath the picture read: *From left to right, Claude Bates and Theodore Ross, convicted in District Court today.*

The item was dated February 18, 1931. An AP dispatch from Urban, Illinois:

District Judge K. L. Mathis today bitterly castigated Claude Bates in passing sentence upon Bates and his convicted accomplice, Theodore Ross, immediately after a jury brought in a verdict of guilty in a case which has attracted wide attention throughout the state and nation.

Charged more than a month ago with fraud in connection with the printing of fake tickets on the Irish Sweepstakes and their wholesale distribution to unsuspecting buyers, the two men have been in custody here in County jail while awaiting trial on the information sworn to by District Attorney Redford Mullins of Urban.

Claude Bates, confessed ringleader in the conspiracy, was characterized by Judge Mathis today as a menace to the community, and severely reprimanded from the bench for having turned his inventive talent to crime instead of applying it to the solution of worthwhile problems.

Denouncing Bates for putting temptation in the way of Ross, formerly a respected businessman in the neighboring town of Fountain, Judge Mathis imposed a sentence of from twenty to fifty years imprisonment upon the older man.

More lenient toward Theodore Ross, who was shown by evidence submitted at the trial to have had no part in the crime except to weakly allow his printing plant at Fountain to be used for illegal purposes, the judge sentenced him to serve from eight to fifteen years in the State Penitentiary at Joliet.

Deputy Sheriff Elisha Hogan will entrain with the two prisoners tomorrow morning for Joliet where the great steel gates will clang behind them, shutting them off from the outside world for many years and giving them full opportunity to consider the oft-repeated statement: Crime Does Not Pay.

Shayne got a cigarette from his pocket and lit it while his eyes raced over the item. He nodded his head slowly as he finished, inhaled deeply, and lifted his head to stare with abstracted eyes at the dead man.

His fingers slowly refolded the newspaper clipping and slid it into his coat pocket.

As he stared at Hardeman, the brooding look of lost hope faded slowly from his eyes. It was replaced by a gleam of fierce preoccupation, of intent concentration, as though he visualized something else, something entirely different from the scene of murder before his eyes.

His nostrils flared widely, then subsided. His features settled back into placid lines of decision as the silvery blast of a bugle came through the window announcing to patrons of the track that the last race of the evening was about to get under way.

He slid his hip off the desk and went to Hardeman's side, studying the position of the body and the hand groping toward the pistol it never reached.

He stepped back and tentatively wormed his toe under the corner of the office rug, turned it back to uncover the bare floor between the swivel chair and desk.

Nodding with satisfaction, his eyes took on a hard brightness. He draped his handkerchief over the back of Hardeman's flaccid right hand, put his own hand over the handkerchief and got a firm grip on the dead man's fingers, which were stiffening rapidly.

He inched the hand gently forward in the open drawer, using extreme care not to change the natural position of the corpse. He pressed Hardeman's fingers about the butt of his own .38 and drew it out.

Careful to allow only Hardeman's fingers to touch the polished steel and corrugated wooden butt, he turned the cylinder and assured himself that the pistol was fully loaded.

He crouched beside the chair, lowered the dead man's hand and gun toward the floor with muzzle down, aimed at a spot of bare wood from which the rug had been turned back.

He cocked the pistol with his handkerchief over the hammer, maneuvered Hardeman's unresisting first finger under the trigger, curled it snugly against the steel.

Sweat streamed from the detective's seamed face as he crouched there at his ghoulish task. He forced himself to wait, his own finger on top of Hardeman's, holding it against the trigger.

There was a lull in the crowd sounds coming in the window; the band ceased playing. It was as though the thousands in the grandstand had an inexplicable pre-science of what awaited in the back office, as though they momently caught their collective breath, stilled the clamor of their voices so that the shot might be clearly heard if Shayne dared to press the trigger.

Into the lull came a faint racketing din familiar to every greyhound fancier. The clatter of wheels on curved rails starting at the far side of the oval track, growing louder as the electrically propelled motor zoomed, forcing the stuffed rabbit to bob around the track in exact simula-tion of the swift bounds of a fleeing jack rabbit.

The dogs set up a yapping in the starting-boxes as the rabbit rounded the turn and came toward them. The yelping of the hounds increased, rising to a shrill cre-scendo as the bouncing bit of fur raced by the boxes.

Michael Shayne waited with his finger tense on the dead finger gripping the gun. Sweat streamed from every pore of his body.

Then it came, surging in through the window. A deep roar that drowned the yapping of the hounds and the racketing of the mechanical rabbit. Two words bursting in unison from a thousand throats:

"They're off!"

Shayne's finger jerked against Hardeman's, pressing the trigger hard.

The sound of the exploding cartridge was loud in the confines of the office, but merged soundlessly into the roar of the crowd outside.

The bullet tore into the pine floor beneath, a small round hole in the planking.

Still moving with infinite care, Shayne shifted his foot and let the corner of the rug fall back into place, covering the single bullet hole in the floor.

He released his hold on Hardeman's hand and the pistol dropped to the rug.

Shayne stood up, mopping his face with the handkerchief which had just assisted him in turning a clear case of murder into a perfect suicide.

He then shook his head slowly. The job wasn't perfect. Not yet. He bent down and pulled the rubber finger tip cover from Hardeman's hand, slid it onto his own right forefinger.

Going to the typewriter, he began hitting the keys slowly and carefully, using only the protected forefinger for operation, pressing the shift key and moving the carriage with a handkerchief-covered left hand.

Beneath the date which Hardeman had typed before he was murdered, Shayne wrote:

I can't go on this way longer. I thought I could get away with it but I was a fool. When Shayne was here this evening

I could tell from the way he looked at me, the way he spoke, that he suspects the truth.

I killed Mayme Martin in her apartment. I had planned it that way from the beginning . . .

Shayne typed on steadily, the clacking of the machine loud in his ears. He ended with the words:

. . . only thing left for me to do. I am going to shoot myself through the right temple and may God in His all-embracing wisdom pity me, though I deserve no pity.

He stepped back from the typewriter and read what he had written, leaving the sheet of paper in the machine. Nodding approval, he stripped the rubber covering from his finger, replaced it on Hardeman's after obliterating all prints from the inside with his handkerchief.

Grateful for the clamor outside, to which the noise of starting motors was added from the parking-lot, Shayne took time for another slow and comprehensive survey of the interior of the office. Changing the setup from murder to suicide had, strangely, made no difference in the appearance of the room.

He went to the door and opened it enough to press the button releasing the night latch, carefully polished the knob and the light switch.

Leaving the door slightly ajar, he strode back to the desk and with his elbow pushed the telephone to the floor from its position on the extreme corner where Hardeman's outflung hand might have struck it as he died.

He went out without a backward glance, leaving the light burning, and as he passed through the door he could hear a metallic voice rasping from the phone on the floor:

"Number, please. Number . . .?"

No one saw him go swiftly down the hall and out under the grandstand, where an eddying mob of people surged toward the exit gates. He joined them, let himself be shouldered around until he reached his roadster, and waited until he was able to edge out onto the highway.

Bright stars gleamed in the sky, covered here and there by fleecy white and scurrying clouds.

He drove slowly, completely relaxed behind the wheel, while a stream of cars raced past him.

The full-bodied scream of a police siren brought him alert as he approached the outskirts of Cocopalm. He grinned briefly as an automobile with red accessory lights and siren going at full blast sped past him toward the greyhound track.

Shayne did not stop at the hotel, but drove a few blocks beyond and turned toward the beach. As he neared Midge Taylor's cabin he saw lights in the windows and Gil Matrix's Ford parked in front.

Will Gentry sat behind the wheel of his car across the street and a block south.

Shayne stopped beside Gentry's car. The Miami detective chief removed a cigar from his mouth and leaned out, gesturing toward the cottage. "Your man pulled up and went in soon after I parked here. Nobody has come out."

"Thanks, Will. I'll take over now." He rubbed his chin thoughtfully. "Will you do me one more favor?"

Gentry said. "I might as well be your errand boy as anything else," caustically.

"Stop by the hotel and ask Phyllis to get a cab and come out here. It'll only delay you a minute," Shayne said mildly, "and then you can drive on out to the track and see what's up out there."

"The track? What is doing out there?"

"I didn't stop to ask anybody but I just saw the Coco-palm police force headed hell-bent in that direction. I would've gone too, but I knew you'd be getting impatient on this assignment."

Gentry growled something unintelligible and put his car in gear, but Shayne detained him:

"I'll meet you at the police station in half an hour with Matrix. Tell Boyle to get Payson and MacFarlane down there too. We'll clear everything up while we're at it."

Gentry nodded and drove away at high speed.

Shayne pulled ahead and parked behind Matrix's Ford. He got out and glanced in the back of Matrix's car. Three traveling-bags and a briefcase were stacked on the back seat.

He went up the shell walk and stepped onto the porch lightly, turned the knob and opened the front door noise-lessly.

Gil Matrix stood with his back to the door and facing the hallway leading to the bedroom. Midge's voice floated in from the room as Shayne stood there.

"I'm hurrying as fast as I can, Gil," she said. "Will I have time to pack another bag?"

From the doorway Shayne answered for Matrix: "Don't bother to pack anything else, Midge. You're not going anywhere."

Gil Matrix whirled around with a smothered curse as Shayne spoke. His eyes glittered and his thin features twitched. He whipped a revolver from his pocket and leveled it at Shayne, called loudly to Midge:

"Sure. Pack another bag if you want to. We'll leave as soon as you're ready."

Chapter Nineteen: ENOUGH MURDER FOR ONE NIGHT

SHAYNE STEPPED OVER THE THRESHOLD, moving with careful ease, taking extreme precaution to avoid any sudden gesture which might cause an instinctive reaction from Matrix's trigger finger.

He frowned at the leveled pistol. "It's too late for that, Matrix. Better put it down before it goes off."

Midge rushed into the room, her face pale and pinched with terror. She stood close behind Matrix, her stark eyes looking at Shayne over the editor's shoulder. She breathed: "What is it, Gil?" Then, "Oh—no!" in a great sobbing breath when she saw the gun in his hand.

"Stand back out of the way," he rasped over his shoulder. "Get your stuff ready. No one can stop me now." Standing perfectly still he appeared to swagger and strut defiance.

Shayne saw Midge tense. Her stricken gaze was fixed on Gil's pistol. She made a quick move with her right hand as if to grab the weapon.

Shayne said, "Don't," sharply.

When she drew back with an expression of disbelief, he explained, "It might go off if you reach for it. There has been enough murder in Cocopalm tonight." He moved sideways, keeping his hands in plain sight, and sat down near the front window.

Matrix did not move. His head was hunched forward between shoulder blades that jutted up on each side. His round, owlish eyes held Shayne's unblinkingly. He warned in a thin high voice of near-hysteria, "There's likely to be one more killing, Shayne—unless you use your head."

"No, Gil," Midge begged. She pressed close against him. "I don't understand," she wailed. Her tongue came out to moisten her lips but left them dry. "You won't tell me anything. What's all this—talk about killing? Why should Mr. Shayne try to stop us from going?" She spoke with great effort and tried again to moisten her lips with a dry tongue.

"Because he's too smart," Matrix snarled. "Because he wasn't satisfied with what was right before his eyes. He had to go digging into something else." The little editor's body began to tremble violently. The pistol was not cocked, but Shayne knew that it had a double-action mechanism and too much pressure on the trigger would fire it without cocking.

Midge put her arm around Matrix's shoulders. Terror drove all youth and gaiety from her face and she looked as old as Gil Matrix. She crooned, "There now, Gil. There now, darling," as a mother might croon to her baby.

She exerted gentle pressure on his shaking body, moving him slowly sideways to the couch. He let himself be pushed down to the cushions. The pistol wavered, then slid from his inert hand to the floor. He looked down at it in some surprise, slowly moved the fingers of his right hand as if testing their ability to move.

When he raised his eyes to Shayne's the desperation had gone out of them and the pinched look had passed from his thin features. He nodded and essayed an odd little secretive smile.

"You win. You and Midge. It wouldn't do for her to go away with me."

"No," Shayne agreed. "It wouldn't do at all—Ross. You should have learned by now that nothing is ever gained by running away from things."

The editor's eyelids flickered at the name of Ross. That was the only evidence of surprise he allowed himself. He said, "So—you know all about that?"

Midge had curled herself up on the couch beside him. She had her arm around his neck and her finger tips caressed his cheek as she gazed at Shayne with bright, questioning eyes, trying desperately to understand without asking questions.

Shayne said, "Yes. I know all about that." He paused, added casually, "I talked to the warden at Joliet long-distance this evening." He took a pack of cigarettes from his pocket and offered Matrix one.

The little editor said, "No, thanks. I don't see how—" He stopped, chewed fiercely on his underlip.

Shayne lit his cigarette. "You don't see how I found out —with Mayme Martin and Ben Edwards both dead—and with you grabbing off the anonymous note Hardeman sent to me at the hotel."

"You—know about that too?"

Shayne shrugged. "I guessed it came from Hardeman. He seemed to be itching all along to tell me something without quite getting around to it. I can make a pretty good guess what was in it."

"Go on," Matrix probed. "Guess."

"He doubtless mentioned your past penitentiary record —and Ben Edwards's. And I imagine he pointed out the proximity of the *Voice* office to the ground-floor windows of the Elite Printing Shop, and mentioned the camera that Ben had invented. I understand the camera had a faculty for taking very clear pictures from a great distance —an invention which would undoubtedly enable you to get pictures of each new set of tickets as they were printed

—to be reproduced by you. And I presume he did not neglect to point out the incriminating fact that Edwards had suddenly decided not to patent his invention—but was resolved to keep it a deep secret even though a patent might be worth a great deal of money."

Matrix nodded his bushy head. "All that was in the message. I was a sap to think it would do any good to keep it out of your hands. I might have known you'd go right to him and get the same information."

"Why, no," Shayne answered placidly. "I admit I just came from the track, but Hardeman wasn't talking."

Matrix stiffened. His eyes were blank as they darted toward the pistol on the floor beside him.

Shayne said again, "It's too late for that."

"Yeh," Matrix agreed in a dull voice. "Yeh. I guess you're right."

Shayne reached in his pocket and took out the old newspaper clipping. He handed it to Matrix, saying, "Here's something you forgot to get from Hardeman the last time you saw him."

Matrix took it from him and started to unfold it, then glanced quickly at Midge and stopped.

"Show it to her," Shayne commanded evenly. "She has a right to see it. Trying to escape your past is what has put you in this trap."

Matrix said, "I guess you're right. I haven't been very fair to Midge. But—hell, a man gets to thinking—" His voice was wooden, without inflection. He handed the clipping to the girl and leaned back against her arm. He closed his eyes while she opened the clipping with exaggerated care and stared at the picture, then swiftly read the text.

It fluttered from her fingers when she finished and both her arms tightened around Matrix's neck. "Is *that* all it is?" she demanded. "Why, that was a long time ago. What do I care? It's nothing—nothing! Every man makes mistakes. Everybody does."

Gil Matrix sat up straight and disengaged her arms from around his neck. "No, that isn't all. You don't understand, honey." He turned to Shayne. "How did you figure all this out?"

"It was easy—once I got on the right track. I expect I got my real clue from the same place Hardeman got his. That deed made out to Gil Matrix by Theodore Ross. It doesn't take a handwriting expert to see the similarity in the signatures. As a director of the bank, Hardeman inspected the papers when you applied for your loan."

Matrix said, "Yes. I guess that was it. I wondered—how he had found out. I've suspected he knew for some time but I was never sure until I intercepted that anonymous note he sent you tonight. As soon as I read it I knew it must be from him."

"Mayme and Ben Edwards were already dead," Shayne mused. "You thought they were the only ones who knew. It must have been a great shock to learn that their deaths hadn't helped any—to know Hardeman also had you dead to rights on the counterfeiting deal."

"I don't know why he didn't present the evidence against me sooner," Matrix said helplessly. "He must have suspected me from the beginning. Anyone would," he ended savagely.

"Your background made you the obvious suspect," Shayne agreed tranquilly. "Taken in conjunction with Ben's camera, which provided a means of keeping yourself informed of the changes made in the tickets each day, no jury would require much time to deliberate your guilt. You tried hard enough to steer me toward MacFarlane," he added parenthetically.

"Sure I did. I knew if you nosed around long enough you'd start turning up the dope against me. That's why I used all my influence to get you called on the case—because I figured you'd go after MacFarlane. God knows, Boyle wouldn't take any action in that direction. I didn't know, though, that Mac would be fool enough to send his boys after you the first thing. That was the tip-off."

"I haven't thanked you yet," said Shayne, "for the picture you sent up to my wife's room. We'll frame it—as a fitting souvenir of one of the damnedest cases I ever worked on."

A caustic smile illumined Matrix's features. "I had to get to Jake and smash that plate. It leaves you in the clear to go on after MacFarlane—no matter what."

"No matter what," Shayne agreed gravely. His eyes stared dreamily at the whitewashed wall of the little cabin as his body relaxed in the wicker chair.

Midge had been listening in silence, pressed close to Matrix. Now she moved and asked nervously, "What picture? Do you mean—?"

"Yes, honey. That's the one we mean. It wasn't your fault," Matrix went on swiftly, "that MacFarlane used you to get a lever on Shayne. You didn't know the ins of it— the spot I was in unless Shayne hung the counterfeiting rap on MacFarlane in a hurry. That was my fault for keeping the truth from you."

"But I still don't understand," Midge interposed. She frowned. "You weren't counterfeiting the tickets, were you?"

Matrix said, "No," hoarsely.

"Then what's all this talk about you being in trouble? Why does Mr. Shayne look so grim and why were we packing up to leave in the middle of the night? Why did you threaten him with that gun when he came in?"

"Ask him."

"*Why*, Mr. Shayne? Do you think Gil was printing the forged tickets?"

Shayne said, "No, Midge. I'm certain he wasn't," in a flat even voice.

Her face brightened and she was young again. "Then why—?"

Automobile brakes ground on the pebbled street and the trio instinctively turned their faces toward the door and listened. A car door slammed. Matrix's eyes dilated. He glanced down at the pistol and his fingers curled toward it.

Shayne said, "No," and shook his head as light footsteps sounded on the porch. He lounged to his feet when a knock sounded, saying, "That will be my wife."

He opened the door and Phyllis entered the room hesitantly, her dark eyes softening as she looked past Shayne at the tableau on the couch. Midge clung to Gil's right arm, pressing her cheek against his shoulder.

Shayne said, "You've both met my wife." He looked directly at Matrix and added, "She has come to stay with Midge while you go to the police station with me."

Midge uttered a little cry of terror. She threw herself across Matrix's chest and clutched him tightly around the neck as though she would never let him go.

Phyllis turned tear-filled eyes away from them. She was trembling as she searched her husband's gaunt face for some hint that it was not true.

His lined features were implacable. He waggled his head from side to side, looking straight into his wife's eyes, then moved past her to stand in front of the pair strained together in an agonized embrace.

Shayne spoke in a curt tone that brought a smothered cry from Midge:

"Hand me that gun from the floor, Matrix, and let's go."

Matrix put Midge from him. She fell back against the couch sobbing wildly, her eyes staring. Phyllis came to her and put both arms around the weeping girl and tried to comfort her. She gave her husband a quick I'll-hate-you-forever-for-this look and did not glance at him again.

Shayne stood his ground with only the lines on his face deepening to give a hint of his true feelings. He said, "It's now or never, Gil. If you love Midge the only thing you can do for her is to come along without a fuss."

Matrix's too-big shoulders were hunched forward, his round eyes staring bleakly down at the revolver on the floor. He reached to pick it up and Shayne made no move to interfere with his actions. Matrix got hold of the weapon with lax fingers, then stood up and handed it to the detective without a word.

Shayne took it and dropped it into his coat pocket. He swung on his heel and went out the door.

Gil Matrix joined him on the porch. They stood there for a moment and the sullen roar of the sea made a dirge-like background for the sobbing of the girl inside the cabin.

Matrix raised one hand in a savage gesture of renunciation. He muttered thickly, "What are we waiting for?" and plunged down the steps.

Shayne followed, saying, "We'd better take my car," and Matrix went to it and got in without another word.

Sliding under the wheel, Shayne backed away. He drove to the business section and as he neared the hotel, Matrix said, "The police station is down this street half a block."

Shayne turned a corner and drove half a block. A lot of cars lined the curb in front of the small police station. He parked beyond them and he and Matrix walked back together.

Shayne looked up to see Timothy Rourke lounging in the open doorway. "Hi, Mike," he called out. "You're holding up the proceedings."

Shayne grinned and shook hands with Tim, introduced Matrix with a wave of his hand, "Mr. Matrix, editor of the Cocopalm *Voice*. Rourke from the Miami *News*."

"What the hell?" Rourke demanded as he shook hands with the local editor. "I thought you had this story on ice for me."

"Matrix is pretty much on the inside," Shayne explained. "I couldn't very well cut him out just to give you an exclusive story. But, where is everybody?" he added with a glance inside the front office, empty except for a uniformed man regarding them uneasily from behind a scarred pine desk.

"I haven't been able to get past the sentinel in blue." Tim Rourke ruefully jerked his thumb toward the local policeman. "The big shots are in back somewhere and my press card isn't worth a damn up here."

Shayne said, "Come on. Get hold of my coattail and we'll crash the conference."

He started toward the rear with Matrix and Rourke directly behind him. The policeman got up hastily, saying, "You can't go back there. Chief Boyle said I wasn't to let no one in his private office."

"Two negatives," Shayne pointed out, "make an affirmative. In his ungrammatical way, Boyle actually meant you were to admit anyone." He kept moving and the policeman stood aside helplessly, knowing in his slow-acting brain that he was being circumvented, but not quite sure how much authority Shayne possessed.

A closed door at the rear had neat gold lettering on it: *Chief of Police.* Shayne turned the knob and walked into a smoke-filled private office and a confused murmur of voices. The voices stopped suddenly as he entered. Shayne nodded curtly to Chief Boyle, who sat behind an oak desk with a typewritten sheet of paper in his hands. He stood aside to let Tim Rourke and Matrix file in behind him, then closed the door in the midst of complete silence.

Chapter Twenty: TWO NEGATIVES MAKE AN AFFIRMATIVE

THREE OTHER MEN WERE SEATED in the private office with Chief Boyle. At the chief's right, Will Gentry held a burning stogie six inches from his mouth while he studied Shayne with a look of frank perplexity on his stolid face. Shayne caught his eye and quirked a bushy red brow at his old friend, but Gentry did not respond. Behind the look of perplexity there was a hint of grim resolution that refused to be easily diverted.

Albert Payson was uneasily huddled in a chair directly in front of Boyle's desk. The village banker appeared shriveled, and his normally ruddy countenance held an expression of shocked horror, of inner disbelief that struggled unsuccessfully against outward acceptance.

Only Grant MacFarlane appeared wholly at ease and happy about the whole thing. He lounged in a chair tilted back against the wall, still wearing his well-cut evening clothes and a look of insolent approval on his finely chiseled features.

Chief Boyle spoke first. He no longer appeared blusteringly aware of his own unimportance and incompetence. Here, in his private office behind his own desk, he was in full command of the situation, and he immediately made it clear that he intended to retain command. He said, "I don't think we need you any more, Shayne. Everything is cleared up."

Shayne said, "That's fine." He glanced out of the corner of his eye at Timothy Rourke and that veteran of many such conferences sidled away unobtrusively, settling himself in a corner with copy paper on his knee, where he could listen and not be noticed.

Shayne took the editor's arm and led him closer to the desk. "I've been having a talk with Mr. Matrix," he explained mildly, "and I think you may be interested in what I've learned."

Chief Boyle cleared his throat and rattled the typewritten sheet in his hands. "I'm afraid you're a little late," he said tolerantly. "I don't know where you've been this last half hour, but you evidently don't know what has happened."

"That's right." Mr. Payson spoke up squeakily. "It looks as though the case has solved itself, Mr. Shayne. I fear you won't be able to take the credit, and—"

"And won't be able to collect my fee?" Shayne finished for him sardonically. "I'm afraid I'll have to disagree with you. I figure I've got the whole thing in the palm of my hand." He glanced from Payson to Gentry, met that same disapproving, unyielding glance.

"I doubt it, Shayne." Chief Boyle was not to be denied. He laid the paper down in front of him and thumped it loudly with his fist. "I guess you don't know, for instance, that Mr. Hardeman has just committed suicide."

Shayne echoed, "Suicide?" in a loud unbelieving tone

to cover a gasp of astonishment from Matrix by his side. His fingers tightened warningly on the editor's arm. He frowned and shook his head. "Why, that's unbelievable. That—changes everything."

"Exactly." Chief Boyle's voice held the exultant ring of triumph.

"Look here," Shayne growled. "That's too damn many suicides to swallow in one gulp. Don't forget that Mayme Martin and Ben Edwards were both murdered and fixed up to look like suicides. How do you know?"

"Hardeman's death is definitely suicide," Boyle snapped. "Mr. Gentry and I made a thorough investigation."

"Is that so?" Shayne glanced at Will Gentry.

The Miami detective chief nodded soberly. "There doesn't seem to be any doubt. Shot with his own gun—and I checked it for prints myself. Hardeman's are all over it—no one else has handled it."

"And he left a note," Boyle put in, tapping the sheet in front of him. "It explains everything."

Gil Matrix cleared his throat. He moved back a step, his eyes warily darting from one of the group to another.

Shayne shrugged his big shoulders. "All right. If you gentlemen are certain Hardeman committed suicide, that's enough for me. But it doesn't change things any. Matrix has a confession to make."

The little editor drew himself up to his full height as five pairs of eyes turned to him.

Mr. Payson leaned forward in his chair, shaking his head. "A confession?" he breathed. "But I don't understand. Mr. Hardeman left a full and complete confession."

"One thing at a time," Shayne growled. He turned to address Chief Boyle directly. "Florida has a state law providing that any man with a prison record must register with the authorities as an ex-felon when he settles here. Mr. Matrix—or Theodore Ross, to be more exact—neglected that detail when he came to Cocopalm."

Albert Payson wet his lips and spread his hands out in a distracted gesture. "Ross?" he muttered. "Then, it is true—"

"He's ready to take his medicine," Shayne said shortly. "Ben Edwards was guilty of the same mistake, but he's already paid a heavier penalty than will be assessed against Matrix."

The thud of Grant MacFarlane's front chair legs striking the floor was loud in the office. He lounged to his feet and spoke to Boyle: "I don't know why I have to be here. Everything seems to be all cleared up."

"Sit down," Shayne ordered. "You're not in the clear by a long shot." He waited while MacFarlane slowly sank back into his chair, then went on harshly: "Don't bank on that picture Jake Liverdink took of me tonight. There won't be any prints made of it." He turned his attention back to Chief Boyle. "You say Hardeman made a confession?"

"He certainly did. Just before he shot himself." Boyle rustled the sheet of paper. "The damnedest thing you ever read."

"Wait a minute." Shayne held up one hand and eased a hip down on the corner of Boyle's desk so he directly faced Gentry and Payson. "I'm about to be gypped out of my fee," he protested. "I was hired on a contingent basis to solve this counterfeiting case. Now, you birds are trying to prove it solved itself—just because Hardeman was a weakling who couldn't stand the gaff when I put the pressure on. That's not fair to me. Hell, I had it all tied up in a knot before Hardeman killed himself. How about it, Will? Won't you help me get a square deal?"

Will Gentry sighed through pursed lips. His eyes rested on Shayne's gaunt face, narrowed and speculative. He nodded slowly in response to his friend's appeal. "I imagine Mr. Payson will be fair about it. If you can prove you actually had the solution and were ready to crack down, I'd say the track is legally responsible for your fee. Don't you agree, Payson?"

"Well—er—yes, I would say so. If Mr. Shayne can prove to us that he was in possession of the salient facts."

"I'll do better than that," Shayne boasted. "I'll undertake to tell you just what was in Hardeman's confession, though you all know I haven't read a word of it."

He lit a cigarette, glancing across at Tim Rourke, who was furiously taking notes. Rourke grinned and nodded encouragement. Shayne glanced from him to Matrix, who still stood aside awkwardly, his shoulders hunched in a defensive attitude, his gaze flickering suspiciously about as though he refused to believe anything he heard. "Take the weight off your feet, Gil," Shayne advised, "while I try to earn seventeen thousand bucks. That's the correct amount, isn't it, Payson?"

"Approximately, yes. Since it appears the track will sustain no further loss after tonight."

"All right," Shayne began slowly, "here's the story. Just for the record, let me say that I first began to suspect Mr. Hardeman at seven o'clock tonight."

He paused, glancing at MacFarlane with an ironic grin. "Though I did also think you might easily be mixed up in the deal. That's what you get for harboring crooks out at the Rendezvous."

"At seven o'clock?" Gentry asked. "You mean that shooting in Hardeman's hotel room?"

"Yep. It stank," Shayne asserted cheerily. "In the first place, I don't believe those birds intended to kill me. They didn't have their guns out when I barged in—else I wouldn't have come out of it alive. If they just planned to slug me—what object would be accomplished? No one would be fool enough to think I'd scare off a case that easy.

"That was the first thing that looked phony," Shayne went on, taking a deep drag on his cigarette. "Then there was Hardeman all tied up in the clothes closet. But the closet door had been left ajar so he wouldn't smother in there. Why? Why were they being careful of Hardeman's health—unless he was the one who had hired them to pull the attack on me?"

"By God," Boyle broke in excitedly, "Hardeman mentions that right here. He realized leaving the closet door cracked was a mistake."

"The only reason I could see for any of it was that Hardeman had fixed that scene to put himself wholly in the clear before the investigation started. By faking an attack on himself he hoped to divert suspicion from himself entirely. His own guilty conscience made him do it, of course, and it served to point suspicion at him instead."

"Why didn't you say something right then?" Payson interpolated with genuine regret. "Ben Edwards might still be alive if you had."

"Hell," Shayne snapped, "that wouldn't have done any good. Where would my proof be? I just had a hunch. I'm sorry about Ben Edwards, but I'm not sure it isn't better this way. If he had lived he would have gone back to Joliet to serve an unexpired sentence. He escaped after serving five years of a twenty- to fifty-year rap."

"That's right, too." Boyle's tone was full of awe. He

tapped a forefinger on Hardeman's confession and nodded. "It's all written down here."

Shayne directed his next explanation to Will Gentry, who had subsided and slumped to a restful position in his chair. "I wanted to talk to Mayme Martin before I started on the case, and made a flying trip back to Miami to see her. I didn't have time before leaving." He paused and grinned sardonically. "I had an important engagement with Mr. Hardeman at exactly seven o'clock." Shayne caught Gentry's eye. Gentry nodded approval. His gaze shifted to Tim Rourke. Rourke's nostrils flared and his eyes twinkled.

"When I got back to her apartment, Mayme Martin was dead," Shayne resumed. "I made the mistake of first thinking she was murdered to prevent her from talking. Then—when Gentry showed me a slip of paper with my name and phone number on it, I began to see it differently. It looked as though she had been *sent* to tell me something that someone *wanted me to know.* You understand, gentlemen, I knew nothing about the case when I talked to Miss Martin. The only name she mentioned was Payson's. She knew, somehow, that Payson intended calling me in on the case."

By way of interruption, Mr. Payson coughed delicately.

"Then I realized," Shayne continued, "what had actually happened. Whoever sent her to me knew that I had been to see her. They didn't know she had demanded money from me for herself and I had refused. Anyone who knows me would know that I would, naturally, refuse." He paused and grinned, catching Will Gentry's eye. "Right here, I would like to exonerate Mr. Payson. Miss Martin's deal was entirely with Hardeman.

"When Hardeman murdered her he was positive that

she had told whatever she was supposed to tell—and her usefulness was ended. Not only that, but she was safer out of the way so she couldn't keep on talking and ball up the deal. So—" Shayne drew his hand across his throat, intimating the manner in which Mayme Martin had died.

"When I learned that Miss Martin and Gil Matrix were old friends and that she had broken with him, it looked like a good bet that her information dealt with Matrix's past—which eliminated Matrix as the man who had sent her to me. He had gone to certain extremes to keep his past a secret."

Shayne sought out Will Gentry's eyes, found them, and winked.

Chief Boyle took advantage of the quiet and said in a loud voice, "Damned if all that isn't right here in Hardeman's confession."

"Now, we come to the part Ben Edwards and his camera played in the case. While I was in Miss Martin's apartment, she called Max Samuelson on the phone and told him she knew for a fact that the invention was perfected and knew where the model and the plans were. This was confusing, as you can readily understand, gentlemen, but the name Ben Edwards stuck in my mind. Remember, I hadn't the faintest idea what anything was about at the time.

"After I arrived here and started working on the case, both Mr. Matrix and Mrs. Edwards tried to convince me that the invention of the camera was not perfected. They gave this reason for Ben's refusal to patent it. I thought he must have another reason, after talking with John Hardeman who assured me that it was perfected. Naturally, I began to bore into that reason. I deduced that there was something in his past which he was afraid would come to light if he applied to Washington for a patent. I know Max Samuelson, and had an idea that he knew what it was.

"I know now what that reason was—Edwards was afraid his real name would come out when the patent office investigated, and he would have to go back to prison."

"Yes, sir," Boyle interjected. "Hardeman knew all that a month ago. He says here that that was when—"

"Wait." Shayne held up his hand with a pained expression on his face. "I've got to convince Mr. Payson I have earned my fee."

"This is all most amazing," Mr. Payson said quickly. "So far as the fee is concerned, I am convinced, but—"

"That was when Hardeman saw what a slick chance he had to put over a counterfeiting deal," Shayne interrupted, "with a perfect frame-up to hang the rap on Matrix and Edwards when the going got tough. I don't know what salary you were paying Hardeman for managing the track," he went on, turning to Mr. Payson, "but it evidently was not enough. He saw the stockholders earning huge dividends while he did all the work."

"That is not true—" Mr. Payson began, but Shayne cut him off.

"The camera and Ben's refusal to patent it must have given Hardeman the idea. It was simple enough for him to arrange with a printer in Miami to print the forgeries. Hardeman was the man who decided what the new design would be each day. He could have his forgeries printed ahead, distributed to the stooges who cashed them for him before the genuine ones were even printed at the Elite shop. And he could get out from under any time he wanted to by letting the truth about Matrix and Edwards's past records leak out. It had to leak out, though, in a way so it wouldn't seem to come from Hardeman—because if it ever became known that he had been in possession of that knowledge all the time he would have had to explain why he hadn't told the authorities at once. Thus, the elaborate precautions to have Mayme Martin tell me—and her death afterward so she couldn't spill the beans about his sending her to me."

"I'll be eternally damned," Gil Matrix rasped out. He spoke slowly and thoughtfully, as if to himself alone, when Shayne paused. "And I thought all the time it was MacFarlane."

"There's still one important fact of the case which you have failed to clear up, Mr. Shayne," Albert Payson warned. "Ben Edwards's death—the murder you accused me of committing."

Shayne chuckled. "I thought you might have—at the time," he told the banker cheerfully. "I had most of the angles figured, but even then I wasn't sure it wasn't you instead of Hardeman. In a way, you have one of the biggest crooks at large to thank for it. I learned from Max Samuelson that Hardeman was out of his office when Edwards was killed. Edwards had been called to his death by a telephone call from some unknown party. Why? I admit I was stuck for an answer.

"Then it came to me. Samuelson was here for the express purpose of paying cash for Edwards's invention. A very little cash, I may say, but we all know Edwards would have accepted the offer. Hardeman knew about it. As soon as Samuelson told him over the phone what he intended to do, Hardeman realized that Edwards's sale of the camera would do away with the mystery it was making of the counterfeiting, and thus discount the value of the camera as evidence against Matrix. Hardeman's nightly revenue from the track would be at an end.

"By that time Hardeman was frantic. He didn't know why I was fooling around and hadn't arrested Matrix—not realizing that Mayme Martin had not told me what she knew. The only out he could see was to kill Edwards before Samuelson got to him with his offer—and to hope the crime would be laid to Matrix when the truth came out—on the assumption that Matrix had killed them both to keep his past a secret and, perhaps, that Matrix could cash in on the camera besides."

"That's right." Chief Boyle nodded wisely. "It's all down here—just like Mr. Shayne says." He looked up at Shayne in frank admiration. "By golly, it's like you had read his mind."

Shayne's shoulders suddenly slumped wearily. "That about clears it up," he said, looking straight at Payson.

The banker wriggled uncomfortably, puffed out his pink cheeks, and nodded. "I see no legal justification for withholding your fee. With Hardeman's confession, the track officials can sue his estate for the amount of losses."

Grant MacFarlane got to his feet and yawned. "None of this evidence touches me in the slightest. I don't know why you insisted upon my presence here. As a matter of fact, I've known about Matrix and Edwards for weeks—and I naturally supposed they were doing the counterfeiting. You remember, I offered you information tonight. Mayme Martin had spilled the whole thing to me one night when she was drunk."

Shayne said, "You can go after I've said this to you. You made a mistake when you got panicky and pushed me around tonight. No man has ever pushed me without regretting it. I don't know what you were panicky about, but I'm going to find out. Pandering to high-school kids is one thing. I'll be visiting your dump again—with authority from the state's attorney in Miami, whom you can't buy off."

He turned away from MacFarlane and the gambler hesitated, his face ashen, then went from the office without a word.

"Come on," Shayne said to Matrix. "You've got a date with a blonde and she'll be getting impatient."

"Now, wait a minute." Chief Boyle lumbered to his feet. "How about this escaped convict business? I guess maybe Mr. Matrix has a date with the state of Illinois."

"No." Shayne shook his head. "Illinois isn't interested. Matrix was released from Joliet in 1936 after serving his term with time off for good behavior."

Will Gentry caught Shayne's arm as he went toward the door. He held him back and Matrix passed them hurriedly, going toward Shayne's roadster. Gentry's eyes followed the diminutive figure and he rumbled, "I hope you know what you're doing Mike."

Shayne said, "I'm absolutely certain." He started to say something else, hesitated as Tim Rourke joined them in the doorway.

"Great day in the mountains, what a mess," the reporter breathed happily. "I don't know whether I'm coming or going with all this thrown at me at once."

"Go back and talk to the chief," Shayne urged. "He'll help you straighten it out into headlines—and how he'll love it."

"Yeh," Rourke said, "you're right." He thumped Shayne on the back and turned away to corner Chief Boyle at his desk.

When they were alone again, Gentry sighed and spoke in a low tone, "From beginning to end I never saw a more

cockeyed case. And tonight, Mike, I saw something I'd
never have believed if I hadn't seen it with my own eyes."

Shayne said, "That so?" and waited.

"A bullet from a Police Positive that had lodged inside
a man's head," Gentry explained. "In thirty years of police work that's a new one on me. A thirty-two will do it
sometimes—but I never thought a thirty-eight would."

"It just goes to show," Shayne told him solemnly, "that
there's always something new under the sun. I'll buy you
a drink when I get back to Miami."

They shook hands with a hard grip that said more than
either would put into words, then Shayne hurried to his
roadster where Gil Matrix waited impatiently.

Chapter Twenty-One: COPS ARE PEOPLE

MATRIX WAITED UNTIL SHAYNE STARTED THE CAR, then said,
"You know I killed Hardeman. Why are you doing this
for me?" His voice was quietly cold, filled with suspicion.

"Because I hate the guts of a louse who cold-bloodedly
plans a crime with the intention of framing another man
for it." His foot pressed down on the accelerator, sent the
speedometer up to sixty. "And when a louse gets stepped
on and the life crushed out of him, I don't call it murder."

"I was—I guess I just went to hell when I read that
anonymous letter intended for you," Matrix confessed. "I
made a mistake when I was a kid. I paid for it. It was too
much to live in terror for weeks—with Midge's happiness
at stake—everything. That's what I went through after
the counterfeiting started."

"Yeh," Shayne muttered. The roadster slid past Edwards's house on the corner. The windows were dark.
Shayne nodded toward it. "There are a couple of other

people who deserve a break."

"Claude was crazy about his wife and boy," Matrix said. "That's why he broke prison, to provide for them. If he knew about it he'd be glad he was dead so his invention could pay them dividends, and I'll see that it does."

Shayne said, "That's all behind both of you now. As soon as a thing is brought out in the open it loses its force. But don't try running away again. Stay here and whip it. You and Midge together can do it."

"We will," Matrix promised fervently. "After what you've done—"

"Don't thank me alone," Shayne said roughly. "Thank Will Gentry too. He knows damned well Hardeman didn't shoot himself."

"I didn't know cops were ever like that," Matrix said in a tight voice. "I never heard of a cop giving an ex-con a break."

"That's hooey. Cops are people." He slid his roadster to a stop behind Matrix's Ford. Window curtains were drawn at the beach cottage and lights burned dimly behind them.

Shayne stopped Matrix as he started up the walk with rapid, short strides. He grunted. "Wait—there's a little formality we need to take care of first." He held Matrix's arm and urged him toward the beach. The tide was going out, leaving a wide expanse of springy wet sand which supported their weight to the water's edge.

Reaching into his coat pocket, he took out the small-caliber pistol. Swinging his arm in a wide arc, he hurled it far out to sea. "If anybody thinks to remove the bullet from Hardeman's head," he said grimly, "you don't want to be in possession of the gun that fired it."

Matrix's body was rigid as he watched the faint splash

as the pistol fell into deep water, beyond where the combers broke. He turned silently and followed Shayne back to the cottage.

Shayne opened the door and beckoned to Phyllis. She sprang up and got her wrap. Outside, Shayne said, "Let's get the hell out of here. I'm beginning to feel like a fairy godfather."

Phyllis had difficulty keeping up with his long strides. "But—what is it all about, Michael? Is it all over? Isn't Mr. Matrix in any more trouble?"

"No more than any man about to be married," he grunted.

"But you—you acted so grim when you took him away, and he was so crushed and tragic. Why, Midge and I both thought he had committed the murders."

Shayne opened the door of the roadster and helped her in. He closed the door and went around to the other side and got in. "That was a test of true love," he explained as he started the motor. "I had to know whether Matrix had the guts to stand up and take it."

"You brute," Phyllis exclaimed, "do you mean it was just a gag—you knew all the time that everything was all right and let Midge think—"

"Something like that, angel. Anyway, you can spend one night in your magnificent hotel suite. I'll have to be here tomorrow to collect a fee from the Cocopalm Greyhound Track."